"I believe when we ___ *and Brandon, she was in his arms and he was having a difficult time controlling his desire for her."*

Isabelle laughed. "Are you planning on narrating everything that happens between us?" she asked.

"Probably not." He brushed his lips against each cheek. "Suspense thrillers are my forte, not romantic scenes, remember?"

"Oh, I wouldn't exactly say that," she contradicted. "You seem to have a very natural aptitude for romantic scenes."

"Nice of you to notice," he told her, continuing to shower her face with tiny, arousing kisses. "I think you should know that no matter what I'm doing, I always try to top whatever I've done before."

"Well then, in the words of the immortal Bette Davis, I guess I'd better fasten my seat belt, because it's going to be a bumpy night."

"Don't bother fastening anything," he instructed. "I'll only have to unfasten it."

Dear Reader,

Brandon Slade is a bestselling author who seems to have it all: looks, money, a sense of humor. He even has a movie icon as a mother. But famous people need loving, too, and Brandon was once married to someone he'd thought was the woman of his dreams, only to have her abandon him and their infant daughter. It made him leery of romantic entanglements and very leery of his own ability to judge a person accurately. All of which makes his mother despair that he will ever get married again.

As for Isabelle Sinclair, she's decided that she's perfectly happy dedicating herself to "fixing broken people." She's a physical therapist who thrives on challenges and brings her own personal brand of enthusiasm to her work. She's in business with her older sister, Zoe, who, like Brandon's mother, worries that Isabelle will never know the joy of having her own family. But once Zoe and Brandon's mother make their fears known to Cecilia Parnell, one third of our Matchmaking Mamas, all they have to do is sit back and wait for the magic to happen. Because it does.

As ever, I thank you for reading, and from the bottom of my heart I wish you someone to love who loves you back.

With love,

Marie

WHAT THE SINGLE DAD WANTS...

MARIE FERRARELLA

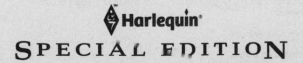

Harlequin®

SPECIAL EDITION

Recycling programs
for this product may
not exist in your area.

ISBN-13: 978-0-373-65604-2

WHAT THE SINGLE DAD WANTS...

Printed in U.S.A.

Books by Marie Ferrarella

MARIE FERRARELLA

This *USA TODAY* bestselling and RITA® Award-winning author has written more than two hundred books for Harlequin Books and Silhouette Books, some under the name Marie Nicole. Her romances are beloved by fans worldwide. Visit her website at www.marieferrarella.com.

To Patience Smith,
who keeps letting me
continue
spinning my stories
in the
school yard

Prologue

Maizie Sommers raised her eyes from the five fanned out cards she held in her hand and slowly scanned the faces of her two very best, lifelong friends, Theresa Manetti and Cecilia Parnell. They were playing poker. The weekly game was the excuse they used in order to take a temporary break from their thriving businesses. They would get together to catch up, share and gossip, although Theresa preferred to call it "a review of local news."

Lately, of equal importance was their continuing passion for matchmaking. And they were good at it.

"So, ladies, any prospects or projects in the offing?" Maizie asked hopefully. Her lively eyes shifted from one face to the other. Faces she knew as well as, if not better than, her own.

The past few weeks had gone by without any of them calling the others, excitedly stating that their services—those outside of the real estate business that Maizie ran, the high-end cleaning service that belonged to Cecilia or the popular catering business that had initially begun in Theresa's kitchen—were once more required.

Cecilia frowned at the hand she had been dealt and separated four of the five cards she held, disdainfully putting them face down on the table.

"Well, I don't know if this constitutes a 'project,'" she began offhandedly, "But Anastasia Del Vecchio was carrying on again about her son's single status. The last time I was overseeing the cleaning crew at her mausoleum of a house, she told me that she would be going on tour in this revival for the next six months. She would *really* love to leave him and her granddaughter in good hands."

Maizie paused, thinking. Remembering. "Her son's that writer, isn't he? The one who writes those bestselling thrillers, right?"

"Brandon Slade." Cecilia supplied the author's name. "I clean both their houses." She leaned slightly forward, sharing a confidence. "Brandon is rather organized for a man. As for her, Anastasia couldn't pick up after herself if her life depended on it."

"She's an actress. It's not part of her repertoire," Maizie commented with a soft laugh. "As for hoping to leave her son in 'good hands,' I'm sure someone as famous and successful as Brandon Slade never lacks for female companionship."

"There's a difference between 'female companionship' and a woman of substance, the kind a man could spend the rest of his life with," Theresa interjected with a knowing expression.

The others knew she was referring to what would

have, until recently, described her son Kullen's situation. The highly successful, handsome young lawyer had once had a different woman on his arm every week. They had arranged things so that he reconnected with the only woman who had ever meant anything to him. A woman, thanks to them, he would soon marry.

Maizie stopped pretending that the cards had any sort of a hold on her attention and placed them all face down on the card table. She slanted a look at Theresa.

"I know that tone. You have someone in mind for Anastasia's son, don't you?"

Theresa smiled. Of the three of them, she was the shyest. But her convictions and loyalties were just as fierce as those her friends harbored.

"Let's just say I have someone who needs to be led to water," Theresa admitted subtly.

"Give," Cecilia ordered, shifting to the edge of her seat and looking at her friend expectantly.

"I catered a lunch for Healing Hands—it's a private physical therapy organization," Theresa explained, answering the silent quizzical looks she saw on Cecilia's and Maizie's faces. "The owner, Zoe Sinclair, said she was worried about her younger sister, Isabelle. She said Isabelle was entirely too dedicated, which was good for the company, but bad for Isabelle's love life—something Zoe said that, as far as she knew, her sister hadn't had in at least a couple of years. Maybe more."

Cecilia sighed. "I know how that is," the woman murmured.

The truth was all three of them did. Friends since the third grade, they had cheered one another on through courtships, marriages and children. And grieved as, one by one, they found themselves sharing yet something else: widowhood.

Eternally optimistic, they believed firmly in romance, which had first caused them to dabble in their daughters' lives, then in Theresa's son's situation. Hooked on the challenge, they were eager to branch out, to help friends and clients who sought to have their children or their siblings find satisfying, lasting relationships. They sought no repayment for their efforts. They did it for the sheer joy of bringing two people together.

Making no response to Cecilia's comment, Theresa produced a candid photograph of her catering client's sister, taken by someone at the party.

With a laugh, Cecilia dug into her oversize purse and pulled out the latest thriller by Brandon Slade, a book he'd given her the last time her crew had cleaned his house. She placed it front cover side down on the table.

"I'll see your photograph and raise you a dust jacket," Cecilia declared, pushing the book to the middle of the table, next to Isabelle Sinclair's picture.

Maizie looked from Brandon to Isabelle and nodded thoughtfully. "Looks to me as if these two young people would make a truly wonderful couple," she agreed, then raised her eyes to look at her friends. "But how do we bring them together?"

That, they all knew, temporarily stumped, was the sixty-four-thousand-dollar question.

Chapter One

Drama was Anastasia Del Vecchio's life. In the spot-light since she'd been three years old, the venerable actress could be forgiven if at times she indulged her inner child and fell back on being a drama queen, some-thing that had been deemed "adorable" by the movie reviewers when she was three, four and five, but seen as a tad grating on the nerves when she hit her teens and twenties.

Ever the trouper, she'd reinvented herself a handful of times since then and was now considered one of the acting world's last true icons.

For the most part, the actress refrained from giving in to this whim. Although, by no stretch of the imagina-tion could the terms "shy" or "retiring" ever be applied to Anastasia Del Vecchio, not even when she slept. At this point in her career, everything about the legendary star was considered to be larger than life. She made a point of greeting both life and people with enthusiastic gusto.

If something couldn't be done in a big way, she saw no reason for it being done at all. Her energetic approach was the hallmark of her life, her five marriages and her numerous affairs. That aspect of her personality would never change. So it was no surprise that when an unexpected fall from the stage where she was rehearsing her latest play necessitated her being rushed off to the hospital, Anastasia was quite vocal about her pain. And she fiercely fought off the suggestion that any sort of drugs be introduced to alleviate her suffering.

"I can *use* this," she declared, batting away the paramedic's hand as he hovered over her with a syringe containing a measured dose of morphine. There were genuine tears of pain in her eyes as she gritted her teeth together. "I can remember this when I have to portray a woman in the throes of dire physical agony."

Anastasia had witnessed too many falls from grace to be complacent about taking any drugs. Drugs would wrestle the control she treasured so highly away from her.

As it turned out, these words were the last the renowned actress said in the ambulance before the pain succeeded in knocking her unconscious.

At the time of his mother's accident, Brandon Slade had been in the midst of wrestling with a completely unfamiliar foe. Writer's block. Like any writer faced with this demon, he had welcomed any distraction. So when the phone had rung, he'd snatched it up and found himself summoned to the theater by a very shaken and distraught director, Tyler Channing. He'd been in his car less than three minutes later and managed to arrive just in time to climb into the back of the ambulance with his mother as the doors were shut.

The paramedic slanted a nervous look at him as he administered the injection to the now unconscious actress. "She always like this?" the man asked.

A fond smile curved Brandon's mouth as he held his mother's hand. "Always."

Brandon Slade, a media darling in his own right, was Anastasia's only child, the product of his mother's second marriage. Head over heels in love, she'd married a passionate Australian actor whose ardor, sadly, was not restricted to the woman he'd exchanged vows with.

Unable to overlook the mounting number of women her husband slept with, Anastasia, with a secretly aching heart, had sent him packing eighteen months into their marriage—and eight months into her one and only pregnancy. The rather pedestrian actor, one Kevin Slade, had made one more appearance to take a look at his son through the nursery window and then disappeared from both their lives.

Brandon was raised by a succession of nannies, some good, some not-so-good. But he never felt the lack of his mother's love even as she wove in and out of his life like a darning needle, taking work close to home when she could, leaving him behind with a nanny and under the watchful eye of her own mother when she couldn't.

Despite this chaotic upbringing, Brandon never felt neglected, never acted out, never felt desperate for attention. For a child born into the acting community, he was a rarity. He grew up centered and well-adjusted. He bore no resentment toward his mother for her less-than-orthodox behavior. She was Anastasia Del Vecchio, and that was just the way she was, a hurricane blowing in and out of his life.

For his part, Brandon enjoyed his life and enjoyed his mother whenever he could. And when he sought to make his own way in the world, there was no one who was more supportive of his efforts—and his chosen field—than his mother. He loved her dearly for it.

Just how much was brought home to him when his own wife had walked out on him—coincidentally before he'd sold his first successful thriller and landed on the *New York Times* bestseller list. She'd told him just as she'd packed up and left that he, and the life he wanted, bored her. He'd been heartbroken and struggling to put the pieces of his life back together, not for his own sake, but for Victoria's. His daughter had been a little more than a month old at the time, and he hadn't known the first thing about taking care of a baby. When she'd heard what had happened, Anastasia had deliberately restructured her life, accepting a lesser part in a cable series that was being filmed in Los Angeles just so that she could be there to help with Victoria.

Unlike some parents when they made sacrifices—and in complete departure from her public persona—Anastasia never made any mention of the inconvenience this restructuring necessitated. She also never told him that she'd passed up a part that landed the woman who took her place an Academy Award. Her best friend, a hairstylist named Olga Newton, had let that little gem drop five years after the fact, which was the only way Brandon ever found out.

Now it was his turn to help her, Brandon thought, still holding his unconscious mother's hand.

As it turned out, the fall resulted in a cracked left hip. When she finally woke up eleven hours later, it was all over but the healing. The horrified actress was less than pleased to discover that she'd had to have emergency surgery and that where there'd once been bone, she now had titanium.

"Like the Bionic Man?" Her voice boomed with displeasure as she absorbed the news.

"Something like that, except you won't be able to run that fast," Brandon informed her, amused. "But the good news is that the surgeon used the newest approach to this surgery on you—"

"You let them *experiment* on me?" Anastasia cried, alarmed.

"Not experiment, Mother. This was a proven method. It's called Anterior Hip Replacement and what I'm trying to tell you is that you're going to bounce back faster because there were no muscles cut with this approach. They were just stretched. You'll be walking by the time I get you home," he promised her.

By this time, twelve-year-old Victoria had been brought to the hospital by his agent and had sat, looking worried, until her grandmother had opened her uniquely violet eyes.

Brandon rested his hands now on his daughter's slight but sturdy shoulders as they both faced his mother with the news. "Oh, and by the way, I'm having your things moved into the guest room."

Anastasia frowned, then sighed wearily. Numbed and a little fearful, she fell back on what she knew. Drama and bravado. "You don't know what things to move."

Brandon took her resistance in stride. He was on familiar ground. "No, I don't," he admitted. "But I'm sure you'll tell me if I've forgotten something."

Sullen, Anastasia reached out for Victoria's hand. Her granddaughter was quick to respond. The role reversal was obvious and unselfconscious. "It's easier just leaving me at home and getting me a nurse."

"You know no one would be able to put up with you on a round-the-clock basis but me," Brandon pointed out, suppressing a grin. "Besides, who will you have around to help smooth out all those feathers you're going to ruffle?" His mother was far from the easiest person to deal with when she wasn't feeling at the top of her game, and this circumstance promised to keep her from that height for at least a month under the best of conditions. Undoubtedly more. "No argument, Mother. It's a done deal."

"I'll disrupt your well-ordered life," Anastasia protested for form's sake. It was easy for Brandon to see that he'd already won the argument. But his mother being what she was, she had to go through the motions so she had something to point to later, should he have a complaint about her staying at his home. "People will be coming and going. Loud people," she emphasized.

"I'll make the adjustment," he promised. "Now, the surgeon said we needed to make arrangements for you to begin physical therapy sessions as soon as possible."

Anastasia balked at the image that suggested to her. "That's for old people," she protested, this time in earnest.

"No," Victoria told her in her quiet, wise voice. "That's for people who take one too many steps backward off a stage."

Also in the room while this verbal three-way tennis match was going on was Cecilia Parnell. Initially just providing a cleaning service, she'd transformed into something more: Anastasia's occasional confidante and friend.

"You know," Cecilia began, "I know the name of an

excellent physical therapist. She's very dedicated and comes with a long string of recommendations," she threw in for good measure.

This was his only mother, and as blasé as he could sometimes sound, Brandon wasn't about to take a chance when it came to the woman's well-being.

"I'd like to see those recommendations," Brandon told Cecilia.

"Oh, Brandon, don't be so uptight," Anastasia chided. "If Celia says she's good, she's good. You want to be useful, make the arrangements," she dictated. Her violet eyes shifted to the woman who cleaned her house to a spotlessness beyond reproach. "They promised me I could go home in two days. See if this miracle lady can be at the house by Wednesday morning. I need to be on my feet—and able to dance—in six weeks. There's a bonus in it for her if she can get me there in less time."

"It doesn't work like that, Mother," Brandon said patiently, exchanging looks with Celia.

"I am filthy rich, Brandon. It works any way that I tell it to work," Anastasia countered with complete confidence.

Cecilia smiled as if to convey how a little miracle was about to be set in motion.

At ten o'clock Wednesday morning, when Brandon opened the door to admit the physical therapist that Cecilia Parnell had recommended, he wasn't exactly certain what to expect. Subconsciously, he had just assumed that Isabelle Sinclair would be a woman of the sturdier variety, big-boned and strong enough to be able to catch an average-size patient. He knew it would probably be viewed as stereotyping, but, like most people, he associated strength with size.

The woman he stared at could probably catch a falling chipmunk. A small one.

He definitely was *not* expecting a petite, delicate young blonde who looked as if she would blow over in the first high wind that blew through the Newport Beach community. So he could be forgiven if he came to the conclusion that this willowy woman on his doorstep was here for some other reason than to begin his mother's physical therapy regimen.

Maybe this was a nurse sent by the physical therapy agency to assess his mother's needs and condition before the actual therapist could be dispatched to begin her work, he thought.

At first, Isabelle didn't recognize him. Oh, she was aware that she was looking up at a tall, dark-haired, charmingly handsome man with a definite boyish streak going for him—and that he was giving her a very deep, thorough once-over almost down to her bones—but she didn't actually recognize his face for at least a good thirty seconds.

And then it suddenly clicked into place.

Of course.

He was Brandon Slade. *The* Brandon Slade, author of—at last count—ten bestselling thrillers. And that was in addition to being the son of the movie icon she'd been sent to work with. She didn't know who she was more bowled over by—her client or her client's son.

In awe of Brandon Slade's talent—she'd read every single one of his books at least once if not more—and definitely not unaffected by his looks, Isabelle Sinclair felt as if she'd just won some kind of fortuitous celestial lottery.

So this is what you meant by saying "Happy Birthday" when you handed me this assignment, Zoe.

At the time, she'd just thought it was her sister's very strange sense of humor kicking in. Now she understood. She was being sent to the home of a writer she admired to work with his mother, an actress who had been her personal heroine when she'd been a child laid up in a hospital bed for an intolerable number of months, thanks to a car accident that had left everyone else with scratches and had all but broken every one of the bones in her body—or at least it had felt as if all her bones had been broken.

Watching Anastasia Del Vecchio take command of every situation she was in had provided her a vicarious thrill—and had ultimately given her a role model to attempt to emulate.

Since the woman in the doorway wasn't saying anything, Brandon asked, "May I help you?"

Oh, God, yes. In so many ways. But, for the sake of decorum, she kept that response to herself, and instead, Isabelle smiled and said, "Actually, I'm here to help your mother, Mr. Slade." Extending her hand to him, she introduced herself. "I'm Isabelle Sinclair. Helping Hands sent me. I'm the physical therapist."

The response came out before he could stop it. "You're kidding."

She looked at him a little uneasily, puzzled by his reaction. "No, I'm not. Why would I kid about something like that?"

This had foot-in-mouth written all over it, but he felt he had to at least try to talk his way out of it. "Shouldn't you be, you know...*bigger?*" He used his hands to emphasize his point.

She smiled, and he immediately noticed that it was

one of those impossibly sunny smiles that seemed to light up a room. The kind of smile that came with its own wattage. Brandon caught himself smiling back.

"Trust me," Isabelle told him, "I'm as big as I need to be, Mr. Slade."

He really had his doubts about that, but if she had any trouble, he intended to be around to lend a hand, so he supposed it was all right.

"If you say so," he murmured. "C'mon, I'll take you to her. She's waiting for you."

Isabelle could feel the butterflies in her stomach multiplying as she followed him. It was a first for her. She'd never felt nervous about meeting a client before.

Brandon led the way to the place his mother was currently presiding over: the living room. Ushering the physical therapist in, he withdrew to give his mother the center stage he knew she both needed and loved.

"I'll be right down the hall if you need me," he told Isabelle in a soft murmur.

The sound of his lowered voice caused a chaotic ripple effect that involved every part of her body. The man was just too handsome for her own good, Isabelle thought.

The next moment, thoughts of the writer's chiseled profile were forgotten as she found herself looking into Anastasia Del Vecchio's violet eyes.

Wow. The single word undulated through her.

"Tell me about yourself, dear," Anastasia instructed with a regal wave of her hand that would have made Queen Victoria proud.

Anastasia was lying on an oversize sofa in the living room, where she had taken up court, choosing to be "in the thick of things" rather than "cooped up" in the guest room, a room that had been sumptuously decorated according to her dictates for those times that she needed to stay overnight rather than return to her own home. The actress lived in a mini-mansion approximately ten minutes away by car—if that car happened to be speeding all the way. And when she drove, it usually was.

As Isabelle appeared to do her best to meet her scrutinizing gaze, Anastasia did a succinct evaluation. Not of a therapist, but of a young woman for whom she had plans.

She had a nice smile, Anastasia thought, and lovely skin and hair, but she definitely needed a little work and patient guidance as far as making the most of her appearance. She supposed that was a good thing. It meant that the girl was dedicated to her work, which was, after all, why she was predisposed to hiring her.

I hope you're right, Cecilia, Anastasia silently cautioned.

This was Anastasia Del Vecchio, Isabelle thought, trying her best not to act like a starstruck groupie. The *Anastasia Del Vecchio.*

She could hardly believe it.

Granted, this was Southern California, and movie and TV stars did cross paths with mortals on a somewhat regular basis, but that didn't make this moment any less awe-inspiring for Isabelle. As a native to the area, she'd encountered more than a couple celebrities herself, but no one of this magnitude and definitely not someone who had captured her heart at a very young age, when fantasy and escape had been so important to her.

"You can speak now," Anastasia told her.

Honesty had always been Isabelle's best strategy. So rather than say she was busy mentally reviewing the woman's case—something she had already done before coming here—she admitted the reason her tongue had remained so unnaturally—for her—dormant.

"I'm sorry, Ms. Del Vecchio, I'm a huge fan of yours—"

Anastasia sat up a little straighter, pleased. Preening. Her eyes smiled first. It was a magnificent sight and she knew it. "Nothing to be sorry about, dear."

"It's just that it's going to take me a few minutes to get used to be being in the same room with you," Isabelle confessed. She did her best not to take any noticeable deep breaths.

Anastasia's pleased smile deepened, going clear down to the bone. "I understand, dear," she sympathized, then tried to lean closer but found that her hip prevented any fluid movements on her part. Silently cursing the impediment, she asked, "Tell me, which of my movies have you seen?"

"All of them."

"Really." Anastasia stretched the word out as she absorbed the young woman's meaning. A slightly canny look came over Anastasia's still amazingly youthful features. After all, Isabelle Sinclair might just be paying lip service, saying what she assumed someone of her stature wanted to hear. "And exactly how many was that?"

Again, there was no reason for Isabelle to even pause to think. She had the answer at the tip of her tongue. She rarely forgot facts she'd learned. "Fifty-three movies, three TV series and two miniseries on PBS," she recited.

Anastasia raised one perfectly shaped eyebrow. "Fifty-two movies," she corrected generously.

"You had an unbilled walk-on in *It Takes Two*," Isabelle reminded her, unfazed.

Highly impressed, Anastasia declared warmly, "You're hired, Isabelle. So when can you move in?"

Isabelle blinked. Had she missed something? "Excuse me?"

"I'm going to need round-the-clock work," Anastasia explained, not accustomed to having to explain herself. "None of this 'an hour here and I'll see you Tuesday' nonsense. I have a play I'm going to be in, Isabelle," she told her with deadly earnest. "I've a key role in the revival of *A Little Night Music.* I sing 'Send in the Clowns,'" she said with a proud toss of her head, adding, "I have put in a great deal of work on this play and I'm not about to have them give my part away to that understudy Channing brought in because of a silly little fall." Her famous eyes became narrow slits as she confided, "She reminds me of Anne Baxter's character in *All About Eve.*"

Isabelle hesitated for a moment. This was an opportunity of a lifetime, and every fiber in her body wanted to shout "Yes!" to the suggestion about moving in for the duration—*my God, living with Anastasia Del Vecchio!*—but it wasn't a decision she could arbitrarily make on her own without at least informing Zoe about it. Otherwise, her sister was going to set her up with other clients as well, and Anastasia apparently intended to monopolize her.

"I'm going to have to check in with my sister, Miss Del Vecchio. Zoe runs the business," she added when the woman looked at her incredulously.

Obstacles were meant to be plowed through, not circumvented. Anastasia had been doing it all her life. "I'm sure it'll be fine with 'Zoe.' I'll pay twice the going rate," she added, confident that would seal the bargain. She took her cell phone out of the pocket of her bed jacket. "Giving me the agency's number, please," she instructed.

It was at that point that Brandon walked back in. Something had told him that perhaps he should come to the physical therapist's aid—his mother could be utterly overwhelming, and the petite therapist brought out the protector in him.

"So, what's the verdict?" The question was directed toward the physical therapist, but it was his mother who answered first.

"She's delightful and she's moving in."

That was twice he was confronted with the unexpected, all in the space of less than an hour. "Run that by me again?"

It hadn't occurred to Anastasia that there might be a problem on either side, especially not on what she considered her end.

"I need her on call, Brandon. I can move back home if you want to play the hermit, dear," she added, knowing that was the best way to get him to agree to her terms. "But my public is waiting and I have to be able to go on tour with the play. We're to leave in six weeks, which means that I have to be able to gracefully and effortlessly walk across a stage in six weeks. Preferably dance across it, but I'll settle for walk." She turned her attention toward the young woman who had been sent to her. "Isabelle here is going to make sure that I am my flexible young self again." She smiled beatifically at her. "Aren't you, dear?"

Isabelle opened her mouth to say that flexibility all depended on how fast the icon's body bounced back and how much and how hard she was willing to work, but she never got the opportunity. Playing all the parts came naturally to Anastasia, so she answered for her.

"Of course she is. Now, the question is, will she be moving in here, or into my humble abode—which does have a little more room," Anastasia added in a stage whisper meant as an aside to Isabelle.

"Of course she can stay here with you," Brandon countered. "I didn't mean I was going to send you packing, Mother, but—"

They were deciding everything on their own, without her, Isabelle thought, acting as if she didn't even get a vote in the matter. And she still needed to inform Zoe of this latest twist. She was fairly certain that there wouldn't be any problem, but she knew that Zoe wanted to be kept apprised of any deviation from the norm when it came to working with a client.

She needed to get a word in edgewise before the conversation got too out of hand. So, taking in a deep breath, Isabelle cried, *"Wait!"* in the loudest voice she could summon, knowing that they wouldn't take note of anything softer.

Surprised by the volume that had emerged from the diminutive woman, both sets of eyes turned toward Isabelle Sinclair. And, at least in Brandon's case, they held a new measure of respect.

Chapter Two

Isabelle Sinclair knew that when people met her for the first time, it usually brought a host of pleasant terms to mind, such as unassuming, laid-back and unpretentious. Those labels, however, did not automatically mean that she was also a pushover or that she was anyone's door-mat. Because she wasn't.

She was so soft-spoken that people were naturally surprised to discover she also possessed a backbone made of steel and the quiet determination of not only the "little engine that could," but the never-swayed-from-his-path tortoise of *The Tortoise and the Hare* fame.

This latter character trait came in particularly handy whenever she worked with clients who were ready to give up and morosely give in to whatever malady had brought them to Healing Hands in the first place.

They might be willing to surrender, but Isabelle wasn't. She wouldn't allow her clients to stop until every single goal laid out was met. Only then, when the disabling condition was conquered, did she feel free to consider the case closed and move on to the next client.

This tenacity also applied to her life insomuch as she would not allow herself to be pushed aside or ignored when the matter directly involved or affected her. And this subject that was being bandied about between mother and son most definitely involved and affected her. More important, it involved Zoe. Nothing brought out her protective instincts more then when someone she cared about was at risk or in need. She considered it her personal mission to come to their aid.

So when Anastasia Del Vecchio and Brandon Slade just took her acquiescence for granted and went on to debate which house would be her temporary place of shelter for the next six weeks, she had to stop them. To that end, she had raised her own voice to far louder decibels than was her custom, effectively bringing Anastasia and Brandon's escalating debate to a skidding halt.

They were both staring at her now as if they hadn't really seen her before. And, from her standpoint, they most likely hadn't. As a rule, on first sight, people tended to regard her as a quiet, reserved shrinking violet. But they soon learned otherwise. She could more than hold her own with the best of them, even if one of those "best" was the dynamic Anastasia Del Vecchio, a woman who could project her voice to the back row of any theater without the benefit of a microphone or any other electronic device.

Two sets of eyes were looking at her, waiting. "I already told you, Ms. Del Vecchio, that I need to check in with my sister and make sure that this arrangement—my living here with you—is acceptable to her. She might have me down for something else."

Anastasia waved a dismissive hand at the words. "Of course it'll be acceptable to her," she insisted confidently. "I said I'd pay you twice the going rate. Three times if I have to," she added. "And since you're going to be here 'round the clock, I'll be paying for your time for that, as well. What businesswoman doesn't like seeing that kind of a profit coming in?" she added.

Isabelle dug in, answering politely but firmly. "I still have to call her."

Anastasia was not above manipulating both circumstances and people to get what she wanted. She could wield basic psychology like a sharply honed sword and had said as much more than once.

"Doesn't your sister like you making independent decisions when it comes to your own work?" Anastasia asked with feigned innocence.

Though he loved her dearly, Brandon knew what his mother was capable of. He didn't like the idea of an unfair confrontation and placed himself on Isabelle's side.

"Mother, I know that you don't know the meaning of the word, but other people do have to follow *rules*. Let Isabelle make the call," Brandon urged—and with that one single sentence instantly became Isabelle's secret hero.

She flashed him an appreciative smile. Not that she wouldn't have called Zoe with the news no matter what Anastasia intended to the contrary, but it was a great deal easier if the woman wasn't attempting to impede her efforts to contact her sister.

And Brandon was handling that detail for her, acting as a diversion and forcing Anastasia to focus her attention elsewhere.

Isabelle turned away from the duo to create the semblance of privacy and called her sister's private cell number.

After four annoyingly long rings, the answering machine kicked in. Isabelle waited as the instructions to "leave a message at the tone" ran its course. The sound of the "beep" made her come to life.

"Pick up, Zoe, pick up." She gave it to the count of ten and then surrendered to the inevitable. "Since you're not there, I'm going to have to make a decision without you. Anastasia Del Vecchio is every bit as dynamic in real life as she is on the screen and she's going to want an answer *now*." Isabelle paused for half a second, trying to think of a reason that would cause Zoe to object to what the actress was requesting. She couldn't come up with a single one. "Okay, she says she wants me to move in with her for the duration of the treatment and is willing to pay up to triple my usual rate, plus expenses. That should go a long way to soothing your bruised ego over having your authority usurped," she said. "You know where to reach me if you decide you want to give me a lecture for old times' sake."

With that, Isabelle terminated the call.

What she'd just said to her sister replayed itself in her head. She still couldn't believe this was happening. It really did seem more like a dream. Anastasia Del Vecchio, her all-time favorite childhood idol, was insisting that she move in with her. Granted, it was in the capacity of a servant—or so the woman thought, Isabelle amended—but the bottom line was that she was still moving in.

Moving in with Anastasia Del Vecchio. It definitely had a nice ring to it.

So did living in Brandon Slade's house, even if he *hadn't* been her all-time favorite author. But he was.

She'd read every one of his ten thrillers, several at least twice. Once for pleasure and once to scrutinize whether or not there were any small holes in the fabric of his plot that she might have missed the first time around. There never were. The man was incredible.

And good-looking enough to stop a woman's heart, she added now.

The call over, Isabelle closed the clam shell, slipped the cell phone into her pocket and then turned around. If Zoe wanted to get in touch with her regarding having her authority cavalierly usurped, to put it in her sister's terminology, all she had to do was call. Her phone was always on.

But for the life of her, Isabelle couldn't think of a single reason her sister would object. Having Anastasia Del Vecchio listed as a former client would do wonders for their references. And their website.

Mentally, Isabelle crossed her fingers that Zoe—once her sister got around to listening to her messages—wouldn't find some flimsy reason to object to her living on the premises.

The moment she'd put the cell away and turned around, Anastasia was on her. "Well?" she demanded, the violet eyes pinning her in place.

"Looks like I'll be moving in for a while," Isabelle replied with a soft smile.

It was obvious by Anastasia's manner that she had expected nothing less. "Wonderful." The actress smiled regally, a queen prepared to be magnanimous with her subjects. "Brandon, why don't you be a dear and show Isabelle just where she'll be staying? And if she needs help bringing her things over—"

Working with this woman, Isabelle thought, was going to definitely be a challenge. If she wasn't careful, the living legend would just roll right over her and flatten her without even realizing she was doing it.

"If you don't mind," Isabelle said, interrupting the woman before the actress got even further carried away, "I'll take a look at the room later. Right now I'd like to get started working with you." Slipping off the light jacket she was wearing, she mentally rolled up her sleeves. "I want to assess just what we need to do so I can work up a proper schedule."

Anastasia didn't see the need for all that foreplay. Not when she knew exactly what needed to be done. "We need to get me upright and dancing, of course."

Out of the corner of her eye, Isabelle caught the smile that curved Brandon's mouth. Ruggedly handsome, he still had very fine features, and his mouth was just short of being described as delicate. Something, she noted, that he had obviously inherited from his mother.

"Good luck with that," she heard him tell her almost under his breath.

And just for the space of a breath, they shared a moment as his eyes made contact with hers—and then he winked.

Isabelle felt the ripple of that wink right in the pit of her stomach. Dedicated and no one's pushover, she was still very much a novice when it came to socializing outside of her work. She could hold her own in any conversation as long as certain parameters were in place. As long as she was Isabelle, the physical therapist, talking to a client or a member of the client's family, she was fine. More than fine. She was sharp, knowledgeable, even witty at times. But always as Isabelle, the physical therapist.

Once that comfortable aura was taken away from her, once she was just Isabelle Sinclair, single female, in a one-on-one situation, she was tongue-tied and self-conscious, at a definite disadvantage inhabiting a world where she had little to no experience.

With effort Isabelle forced herself to clamp down on her reaction to the wickedly handsome writer and focused on the one reason she was here in the first place. To get Anastasia Del Vecchio "upright and dancing."

"All right, Ms. Del Vecchio," Isabelle said briskly. "Let's get to work and see what you can do."

Forty-five minutes later, Isabelle knew exactly what her client could do. She could hit high Cs as she registered her distress each time pain—or the promise of pain—shot through her.

The last, particularly loud, protest had brought them an audience. A very concerned-looking audience.

"Gemma, are you all right?"

The question came from a worried-looking young girl who appeared to be around fifteen. Victoria Slade was actually younger. Twelve going on twenty-one was the way her father had described her in a recent interview, done in the name of publicity for his last book.

Mature in a way that young ladies had been decades ago when such development was necessary, Victoria was the light of both her father's and her grandmother's lives, and neither made any secret of it. Incredibly enough, Victoria continued to be exceedingly levelheaded.

"Gemma?" Isabelle questioned, looking quizzically from the girl to her client, waiting for an explanation as to why Victoria referred to her grandmother by a name that wasn't hers.

Loving any sort of audience, Anastasia complied. "When she was little, Victoria couldn't say 'Grandmother.' Or even the shorter, somewhat mundane name,

'Gamma.'" Anastasia sniffed, clearly at odds with the label. And then she smiled as if the end of the story symbolized some sort of breakthrough. "'Gemma' was the closest she could get. So I became Gemma." Finished, Anastasia briefly laced her fingers together in her lap, then turned toward her granddaughter to finally answer the girl's initial question. "I'm being tortured, my darling. But other than that, I'm fine."

There was love here, Isabelle thought. She could hear genuine affection in every word the famous actress uttered when speaking to her granddaughter. Heard, too, that affection being reciprocated in spades.

The girl with the long, flaxen hair nodded, as if taking the explanation seriously.

"As long as I know," she murmured. Then Victoria walked up to the one person in the room she didn't know and introduced herself. The smile on her lips was a direct copy of her father's, except that there was a shred of shyness woven through it. "Hi, I'm Victoria Slade."

Isabelle was accustomed to children who made noise when they played and had to be physically ushered out by a family member in order not to get in the way.

Impressed, Isabelle took the offered hand and shook it. "I'm Isabelle Sinclair, your grandmother's physical therapist."

"She's going to have me dancing around the stage," Anastasia announced happily, then added with a studied pout, "once she gets tired of torturing me."

"That torture is going to be what helps get you supple so that you *can* dance around the stage," Isabelle informed the older woman in a patient voice.

The actress's goal was a lofty one. Most patients only wanted to be able to walk without a limp. But it was always good to have something to aspire to, Isabelle thought. The line from a poem by Robert Browning floated through her head: *A man's reach should exceed his grasp or what's a heaven for?* applied to both men *and* women.

Victoria, it seemed, had appeared just at the right moment. They would stop here. "All right, I think that's enough for our evaluation session," Isabelle told the woman.

Already back in a horizontal position on the sofa, Anastasia sighed dramatically and fanned herself with a magazine from the coffee table. One that, conveniently, had a flattering photo of her on the cover. The caption, Beloved Icon Down But Definitely Not Out, ran along the bottom of the cover.

"Thank God," Anastasia declared. "I don't think I could have gone on another moment."

She not only could have, she would have, Isabelle thought. The woman wasn't fooling her. She was a born trouper—even if there had to be a lot of noise and fanfare accompanying her every effort.

"By the way, Ms. Del Vecchio," Isabelle began, her eyes sweeping over the woman's long, still very attractive legs, legs that had once been the subject of an enamored famous stage actor's poem. The man had gone on to become one of the actress's many lovers, if she remembered correctly. "Where are your white cotton surgical stockings?"

Anastasia looked down at her legs as well, as if she expected the subject under discussion to suddenly materialize. "You mean those hideous white, cottony things they gave me in the hospital?"

"Yes, those hideous white, cottony things they gave you at the hospital," Isabelle repeated patiently. "Where are they?"

The actress gestured carelessly toward the back of the house and the general vicinity of the room she was presently sleeping in. "In the wastebasket in my bathroom. I threw them away," she added needlessly.

Isabelle had suspected as much. She looked at her client pointedly. "You need to *un*-throw them away," she informed the woman firmly in her soft, gentle breeze of a voice.

"Why?" Anastasia asked. "They make my legs look chunky and so—so old lady-ish," she complained disdainfully.

Okay, more patience, Isabelle silently coached herself. "The stockings aren't meant to be worn as some kind of a fashion statement, Ms. Del Vecchio—"

"Anastasia," the actress insisted.

Isabelle deliberately ignored the slight thrill that had just zipped through her—she was on a first name basis with the great Anastasia Del Vecchio!—and focused on the fact that she had a very stubborn, very willful client on her hands.

"The stockings are meant to help you bounce back faster. And to make sure you don't develop any blood clots."

The magnificent violet eyes narrowed. Anastasia needed convincing. "Really?"

Rather than launch into a long and tedious explanation, Isabelle merely repeated the single word the actress had just said, uttering it with conviction. "Really."

Another huge, resigned sigh escaped the near perfect lips. Anastasia Del Vecchio was no one's fool, and she knew when to retreat. It was how she went on to fight another day.

"Oh, very well." She shifted in her seat to get a better view of her granddaughter. "Victoria?"

Victoria was on her feet. "On it, Gemma," the girl responded. As she turned on her heel and passed Isabelle, the girl said in a low, congratulatory voice, "Score one for your side."

Isabelle couldn't have explained why the approving words pleased her so much—after all, they were coming from a child—but they did.

Several minutes later, the girl returned with the crumpled white cotton stockings. Isabelle took them from her and proceeded to carefully slip them, one at a time, on her patient.

Once they were back on, Anastasia eyed the knee-high stockings with more than a little contempt. "You're sure about this?" she asked Isabelle.

"Very sure," Isabelle answered firmly as she anchored the second stocking in place with what could have once passed as a garter belt. Unlike the ones that were advertised on the pages of catalogs highlighting a thousand and one ways to seduce the man in your life, this particular item was *not* the last word in sexy.

Finished, Isabelle stood back and smiled. "You did very well for a first time."

Anastasia looked at her as if there could be no other outcome. "Of course I did."

The woman gave new meaning to the word *confidence,* Isabelle thought. Uncertain how to respond, Isabelle decided the safest reaction was to smile and then go on to a different subject.

"Well, if I'm going to be staying here for a while, I'd better go home and throw a few things together." She picked up her purse and began to leave the room, heading for the front door.

"You are coming back."

Even though the sentence was more of a statement

than a question, just for a split second Isabelle thought she heard a sliver of uncertainty in the woman's voice. She supposed that Anastasia had her share of people who, unable to take her larger-than-life personality, had abruptly fled her employ.

Not gonna happen here, Isabelle thought.

"Nothing could stop me," she assured the actress—and was rewarded by the return of the woman's confident, brilliant smile.

"Tell Brandon I said to help you," she called after Isabelle.

Right, as if she was about to do that. Out loud Isabelle said, "I'm sure he's busy, Ms. Del Vec—Anastasia. Besides, there's not much to pack. I shouldn't be too long."

She thought she saw the actress smile again in response. With just a little luck, this would work out well, Isabelle told herself.

As she left the room and turned toward the foyer and the front door, she came within a quarter of an inch of slamming right into the very man the actress had told her to summon for help.

The close call abruptly launched her heart into double time.

Chapter Three

Caught off guard, Isabelle swallowed a scream as she stumbled backward. Her heel caught on the corner of a scatter rug that had been thrown down on the travertine floor without, apparently, regard for exact placement. It moved beneath her heel, ripping away the last shred of her stability.

As she tried to regain her balance, there was every indication that she would completely embarrass herself by falling. At the last moment, she was saved from her projected fate, not to mention from sustaining some very colorful bruises in hidden places, by two very strong hands that grabbed her, one clamping down on each of her slender arms.

The air whooshed out of Isabelle's lungs, not because of the sudden, jerking movement forward but because of the close proximity that had unexpectedly material-ized after the save. She found herself approximately four, perhaps five, inches away from the novelist's very handsome face, classic cheekbones and all.

Brandon smelled faintly of some kind of musky cologne or shampoo, and she would have said "sex" if it didn't sound so utterly insane. Her heart slammed into her ribcage, then did a little back and forth ricocheting before finally just settling into an unnervingly fast tempo.

She would have liked to have blamed this erratic rhythm on the sudden jolt to her torso, but she knew better than that. She was athletic and agile and could sprint long distances without really getting winded or breaking much of a sweat.

It wasn't the jolt but the man causing it that was responsible for the uneven, wild beat that had taken possession of her body.

Amused, Brandon grinned at her. "I didn't think that I was that scary."

Completely lost in the jungle of her thoughts, Isabelle blinked. Replaying his words failed to bring any sort of enlightenment or clarity. "Excuse me?"

"You screamed," he reminded her. "I didn't think that I was that scary to look at."

Now it made sense—sort of. The man had to have looked in the mirror in the past decade. After all, he did shave.

"Oh, no, no, you're not. You're very good-looking. I mean—" This was becoming one of those nightmares she used to have where she discovered that her clothes were disappearing, piece by piece, from her body. She could usually make herself wake up before she was entirely naked. But this time she couldn't wake up because she wasn't asleep. She was just making a fool of herself.

Taking a breath, doing her best not to stare at the way his mouth curved invitingly as he smiled, Isabelle tried again. She cautioned herself not to sound like one of those vapid airheads who fawned over celebrities and resembled zombies as they followed them from place to place.

"I'm sure you've looked into a mirror lately," she managed to say more calmly. "You know what you look like."

Her body temperature rose a full ten degrees as his smile deepened and traveled straight to her gut, swirling about like a corkscrew.

"Oddly enough, I find I really don't have the time to spend staring into mirrors." He held up his hand just in case she was about to contradict him. "And before you bring up the obvious subject of shaving, my mirror is usually pretty cloudy from the steam when I shave in the morning. Most of the time I do it in the shower," he clarified. "I've got a little mirror attached to a shower rack."

The thought of Brandon, standing naked and dripping in the shower as he shaved, succeeded in transforming her already wobbly knees into something that would have made Jell-O appear rock solid by comparison.

Heat swept around her, threatening to burn her into a crisp.

Get a grip, Isabelle. You're good at what you do, you're a sensitive, caring, busy physical therapist, not a mindless groupie with no life. Stop acting like one.

That was only half-true, she realized ruefully. Granted, she was a topflight physical therapist—she was always taking classes to keep up on any new, ground-breaking techniques rising up in her field, not to mention absorbing any new theories coming down the pike—and she wasn't by any stretch of the imagination a mindless groupie, but she also had no actual life outside of her work.

How else could she agree to just pick up and deposit herself here, in her client's home, without so much as a minor hassle, other than what clothes to pack and what to leave behind?

After this assignment, Isabelle promised herself she would take some time off and *do* something. *Go* somewhere. Anywhere. Just so that she could say she had gone.

Pulling together her thoughts, Isabelle forced herself to focus on the conversation and not on the fact that she could, at this very close proximity, actually *feel* the heat coming from Brandon's body.

Or, at least she thought she did, which, in this case, was just as bad.

"You just startled me, that's all," she said, addressing the explanation to his shoes. It was easier than looking into his brilliant blue eyes. "I didn't expect to find anyone in the hallway."

He continued to look amused with her. "You always scream when you're startled?"

"Actually," she replied truthfully, "I don't scream. This was my first time."

He would have laughed at her expression if it wouldn't have hurt her feelings. "Well, then, maybe we should go somewhere to discuss this," he proposed with as straight a face as he could manage. "First times are special. Or so I've been told."

Why was it that every single one of Brandon's deep, modulated words felt as if they were cascading slowly down the length of her skin, like the gentle fingers of a questing lover?

Not that she would know firsthand what that was like, she thought ruefully. But she did have a very vivid imagination and could *think* herself into that sort of a situation.

Oh, no, you don't.

Isabelle took another deep breath. Something else she was going to do on that vacation she would take after this. Find out what it felt like to have a lover. Even if it was only for one wild, hot, mind-boggling weekend.

She was tired of wondering what that felt like—to have a man caress her, cherish her, make love with her. If things didn't change in her life and soon, it was only a matter of time before someone snatched her up, stuck her on a plate and put a glass dome over her, displaying her as the last living twenty-eight-year-old virgin in captivity.

She forced a smile to her lips, hoping she didn't look like some kind of a grinning idiot to him. How long before she became immune to the fact that he was Brandon Slade, famous writer?

Probably a lot faster than she would become immune to the fact that, no matter from what angle she looked at him, Brandon Slade was nothing short of drop-dead gorgeous.

It would be one thing if the man was handsome in a sterile way. This was Southern California, and there were gaggles of pretty boys everywhere, looking to make a name, or a career, for themselves. If you looked at one of them, they might be momentarily breathtaking, but there was nothing behind the eyes. They had no more depth to them than a thimbleful of water.

But Brandon, Brandon was another story entirely. Brandon was warm-handsome. Friendly-handsome.

There was something incredibly boyish and appealing about him. Some special x-factor in addition to the man's chiseled chin, high cheekbones and bone-melting sky blue eyes that undermined her entire foundation and reduced her to a pile of sand.

She needed to get over that, Isabelle reminded herself. Or he would think she was some kind of an airhead and ask for her to be pulled from his mother's case. Not that she would have blamed him. After all, she wouldn't have wanted an airhead in charge of her mother's therapy right after her hip surgery either—if she *had* a mother, which she didn't. Not for a very long time, she recalled with the same heavy heart she felt every time she thought of that hole that her mother's death had left behind.

"I'm afraid I'm going to have to take a rain check on that celebration," she deadpanned, playing along with what he'd just said. "I need to get to my apartment and pack a few things if I'm going to stay here awhile." Isabelle glanced at her watch to see what time it was. "I'm sure your mother is already expecting me back."

He laughed softly. "You show promise, Isabelle Sinclair. Only here a couple of hours and already you've gotten to know Anastasia well." He found himself liking this down-to-earth girl-next-door that the physical therapy agency had sent. It was rare to find someone good who was also sensible—and could get along with his mother. "My mother has many attributes, but patience was never listed among them," he admitted.

She liked the way Brandon said her name. Hell, with a voice like that, she would have liked the way he read the supermarket bill, she thought ruefully.

She was doing it again, she chided herself silently.

She was making noises like some love-struck groupie, and that *had* to stop.

Just as soon as the man stopped being so perfect.

No one's perfect. He's got flaws—somewhere, she told herself.

This wasn't like her. She had to snap out of it and start moving, her inner voice argued.

Words found their way to her lips. Finally. "So then I should get going," she told him.

She'd taken exactly two steps toward the front door when she heard him say, "Why don't I come with you?" Surprised, she turned around to look at him. He was already walking toward her. "In case there's any heavy lifting involved."

He probably didn't understand that not all women had the inclination—or the money—to go on shopping sprees.

"I don't own enough clothes to create any heavy kind of lifting," she told him. "I just thought I'd get a few changes of clothing and a few books to read at night."

She saw no reason for the last part of her statement to bring such an amused grin to his lips. "You're an optimist I take it."

Her eyes narrowed. "Excuse me?"

"Thinking that you'll have the time and the energy to read at night," he explained. "Mother will take up most of your time. She has a habit of monopolizing people," he told her. It wasn't a criticism or a complaint. It was just the way things were. It certainly didn't detract from any of the affection he bore the woman who had given him life. "She loves having audiences and you will be brand-new, virgin territory for her."

In response to his words, Brandon saw the deep

pink blush creeping up the woman's neck and face at a breathtaking rate.

Was that his fault? "I'm sorry, did I say something to—"

"No, no," she said, cutting him off before he could begin guessing at the reason she wasn't able to hear the word "virgin" without feeling some sort of personal failure on her part. She told herself that she really didn't care that she wasn't part of a duo, that she'd never really been with a man in that very special way that counted.

That sort of thing bothered Zoe, but not her, Isabelle stubbornly maintained. But it *did* bother her to be regarded as some kind of oddity in this very progressive, outgoing society where couples met on an elevator, and by the time they reached the ground floor, they were hermetically sealed to one another in a passionate, fiery embrace that only promised to be more so once they had some privacy.

"It's just warm in here, that's all." To add weight to her argument, Isabelle pretended to fan herself with her hand.

"I guess you're more hot-blooded than me," he told her.

She looked at him for a long moment, trying to ascertain if he believed her or was just having fun at her expense. She couldn't tell and gave up, hoping it was the former.

"Anyway," he continued, "things go twice as fast with an extra set of hands helping and you'd be doing me a favor."

How could helping her pack be doing *him* a favor? "Oh? How?"

"Well, if I'm helping you get your things together, I've

got an excuse for not sitting at my computer, working," he confided. "Or, in this case, suffering," he added.

She stared at him, completely confused. She'd read his interviews. The man *loved* what he did. So, how could he refer to it as suffering? Was that just for show?

"Don't you like writing?" she asked him.

"No. Well, that didn't exactly come out right," he said, reexamining his one-word response. "I like coming up with the idea, love jotting things down in the middle of the night as they come to me like storm troopers parachuting out of the sky. These are all things that I'm *going* to write," he emphasized. "I also like having written something—you'll note the past tense," he pointed out. "Love rereading the finished product. Tweaking here, fixing there, making it all sound better, ring truer. That part I *absolutely* love," he said with feeling.

"But the actual writing process—the sitting there, staring at the empty screen and desperately searching for the right words or semi-right words to finally fill up that awful, empty screen?" It was a rhetorical question. "No, can't say I like that part of it. Nope, not at all," he declared with a shake of his head. "That's the agony part of this whole gig I'm in. It's pretty much like—well, like sitting down at the computer, opening up a vein and just bleeding."

When he put it that way, it seemed positively awful. "Doesn't sound like something anyone would want to do willingly," Isabelle observed.

He nodded his agreement. "Glad you see my side of it. So, can I come along?" he asked.

He was actually asking her to "tag" along. Boyishly and charmingly asking her. As if he thought there was a chance in hell that she would possibly consider telling him no.

Was he kidding?

What woman in her right mind would say no to him? Especially when he looked so damn appealing asking the question.

"Are you sure your mother won't mind being left alone like this?" she asked.

"She's not alone," he corrected her. "Victoria's here."

He was referring to his daughter. She'd always liked that name. It sounded so regal, so cultured. Unlike her own name which struck her as just being sturdy. Isabelles were the workers of the world. Victorias, on the other hand, were the princesses.

Isabella was the queen who gave Columbus money, and he discovered a brand new world, remember? she reminded herself. *Without Queen Isabella you wouldn't be standing where you are.*

It made no difference.

"Your daughter," Isabelle said with a nod.

"You've met Victoria?" he asked, surprised. Funny, Victoria hadn't said anything, and up until now, his daughter told him everything. He was going to miss that when she hit her teens and became a card-carrying stranger for the next x-number of years.

"Yes, she came in just at the tail end of my evaluation of your mother's condition. She looked more poised than she did in that photograph I saw of her in *People Magazine*."

It took him a second to remember the article the therapist was apparently referring to. "Oh, right. The four-page spread last year," he recalled, nodding. "That was written just as *And Death Do Us Part* came out," he recalled. "Victoria was eleven when it was written, and as she likes pointing out, she's 'matured' since then."

And was in oh such a hurry to grow up, he thought

as a sadness tugged on his heart. He knew he couldn't keep Victoria a little girl forever, but he'd secretly been hoping that he was going to find a way to slow time down. No such luck.

He smiled at the very thought of his daughter. He'd fallen in love with her the first moment he saw her—and could never understand how Jean, his ex, could have walked out on her. But that was Jean's loss, he thought. Right from the beginning, he'd made sure that Victoria would never feel as if she'd been abandoned—the way he had been. His ex-wife's cavalier behavior had left a scar on his heart, but from that first moment, he was determined that it would do no such thing to their daughter. He liked to believe he had succeeded.

"She keeps me on my toes," he confided. "And her grandmother on hers. I'd say that of the three of us, Victoria's easily the oldest one." He laughed, shaking his head. "I don't know if that speaks well of us or not, but it makes my mother happy. She has no use for numbers unless they apply to box office takes or residuals from previous airings. Definitely not when they apply to something as 'mundane'—her word—as age."

As Isabelle listened to him talk, she had to struggle not to get lost in the sound of his resonant voice.

Emerging from her semi-euphoric fog, she suddenly realized that, if he accompanied her, the writer would, perforce, wind up seeing her apartment. That instantly sobered her.

The idea of having someone like Brandon Slade over to her small, crammed flat when he lived in a house that could easily accommodate half a dozen of her apartments didn't exactly thrill her. She didn't consider herself vain, but neither did she like to appear poor or become some kind of an object worthy of his pity.

Isabelle bit her bottom lip, thinking. Maybe she could talk him into staying in the car while she threw a few things into a suitcase.

He's a man, not a pet to leave in the car while you run an errand. Besides, it's hot today, unseasonably hot. You want him to get sunstroke?

You're not supposed to be vain, remember? Especially when you have nothing to be vain about.

Having convinced herself, she lifted her head again, summoning a bright, breezy smile to her lips as she looked into his eyes and said with all the cheerfulness she was able to muster, "I'd love for you to come and help me pack, Mr. Slade."

"Brandon," he corrected automatically. "And you lie very smoothly," he told her in a tone he could have used to compliment her choice in shoes.

Brandon took her arm as if they'd been friends forever and guided her toward the door. The grin he gave her was equal parts sexy, mischief and sunshine.

The latter felt as if it was just bursting through her, giving light to all the dark corners she possessed.

Her stomach bunched up again just as Brandon made a prophesy based on his last assessment of her ability to bend a lie to sound like the truth, something he did on the pages of his books time and again.

"Know what, Isabelle Sinclair? I've got a feeling that we're going to get along just great."

With all her heart, Isabelle fervently hoped so.

Chapter Four

Instead of following her in his own car, the way she had assumed that he would, Brandon walked with her to her car and gave every indication that he was planning on accompanying her to her apartment in *her* vehicle.

Isabelle took an immense amount of pride in her little car because—apart from it being economical and reliable, as well as, in her opinion, "cute"—it was also the very first *new* car she'd ever owned. Every other one she'd driven had been secondhand, time bombs, for the most part, waiting to go off.

Those details not withstanding, she didn't see why Brandon would choose to ride shotgun in her car. Since he was somewhere between six-two and six-four, and the vehicle had obviously been manufactured with passengers no taller than five-nine in mind, seating promised to be severely cramped for the author. Even when he pushed the passenger seat back as far as he could before attempting to get in.

"Are you sure you want to do this?" she asked him uncertainly.

"I'm game," he told her as he began to fold himself up and angle his way into the limited space. It took a bit of doing, but he finally managed to get his entire torso inside the vehicle. As he contorted his arm to get the seat belt's metal tongue into the slot, he cracked, "By the way, when's the rest of the car coming?"

This was *not* a good idea, Isabelle thought. "I'm sorry. When I bought it, I wasn't expecting having someone your height getting into it. I hope you're not too uncomfortable." Even as she said it, she knew he was. He made her think of an early Christian martyr, doing penance.

Brandon began to wave away her concern and discovered that he really couldn't—at least, not literally. There wasn't enough space available for him to execute the movement.

"Don't worry about it. This is roomy compared to some of the seats on the rides I've gone on with Victoria. There was one once at Jamboree-land where I thought I was going to have to fold my legs up around my shoulders, if not over my head."

She'd begun driving the second he'd managed to close the passenger side door. "You don't live very far away, do you?"

"You don't consider Oxnard far away, do you?" The unguarded look of dread that slipped over his face had her hastily negating her response. "I'm kidding, I'm kidding," she assured him with feeling. "I'm just up the road in Bedford."

"Bedford," he repeated, letting the city's name sink

in. He took as deep a breath as he was able, under the circumstances, and released it. It was a lucky thing he wasn't claustrophobic. "Okay. That's not far."

She wasn't sure if he was agreeing with her or actually saying that in an attempt to comfort himself.

"Not far at all," she promised, stepping on the gas a little more aggressively.

The needle on the speedometer jumped to reflect the increase.

Brandon slapped both hands on the dashboard, bracing himself as the speed kept increasing. Glancing at the numbers on the gauge above the steering wheel, he saw that she had passed the speed limit and was now on her way to liftoff.

"You don't have to break the sound barrier to get us there," he told her. "I can play the part of a pretzel a little while longer if it means you won't get a ticket from some revenue hungry motorcycle cop."

Because it seemed to make him just a tad nervous, Isabelle eased her foot off the pedal, but only marginally. "Don't worry, I always watch for them in my rearview mirror."

He wouldn't have pegged her for a speed demon. "Get into many accidents?"

One eye on the road, the other on her rearview mirror, Isabelle shook her head. "Not yet."

"Impressive," was the only word he could summon for the situation.

Within a short amount of time, Isabelle was taking the freeway off-ramp and making her way to the garden apartment complex she'd called home for the past couple of years. It wasn't located very far from the main thoroughfare.

The white daisies that had been so plentiful on both sides of the entrance less than a month ago were now bowing their heads listlessly, surrendering to the hot mid-July sun. Even the asphalt path within the recently painted development threatened to be sticky upon contact in today's heat.

As she drew closer to her ground floor apartment and the carport that stood directly opposite it, noise from the pool area some hundred yards away behind her own apartment grew progressively louder. It seemed as if anyone who was home at this time of day had opted to find some sort of relief from the heat in the complex's large pool.

It was predominantly a very young crowd that took up residence in the Sunflower Creek Apartments. Mostly they were students or recent graduates just starting out in the business world. At twenty-eight, there were days Isabelle felt like an old-timer here. She was definitely one of the older tenants, if not *the* oldest one in the complex.

She felt rather out of sync with the other tenants because she rarely had time to mingle with her neighbors and had ignored the one or two flyers that had been jammed between her doorknob and the wall, inviting her to an "all-night party" at the pool.

The parties were usually scheduled to begin the moment that the complex managers closed their office and went home. The rentals were handled by a retired couple who had nothing in common with the people they accepted as tenants. The duo usually left at the first sign of dusk, which the renters, as a whole, considered fortunate. It was a crowd that loved to party.

Pulling up into her space, Isabelle began having second thoughts about the wisdom of what she was doing. Not about accepting the job—she both needed and wanted that—or even about moving into Brandon Slade's cavernous home for the duration of his mother's therapy sessions. She'd already decided that might even turn out to be fun. Lord knew living on the premises would be a great deal less stressful than hopping into her car every morning and bucking the commuter traffic as she worried about not getting to the session on time. There was nothing she hated more than being late.

No, the wisdom she was doubting was in bringing Brandon here, to what had to seem like a doll-size apartment. He'd probably think she was some kind of pauper. She didn't see herself that way, of course. She was frugal, and she knew how to live within her means. But to Brandon Slade, she had to seem like someone who was about two steps removed from a homeless shelter.

She did *not* want to be the object of the man's pity. But how could she not be? After all, look at where he lived. The house could easily have a railroad running through it, and it would go largely unnoticed.

Getting out of her car, Isabelle waited for Brandon to pull himself out of the passenger side. She did what she always did when she anticipated something uncomfortable coming her way. She tried to head it off at the pass.

Leading the way to her door, she unlocked it, and, as she allowed him to walk into her apartment first, she made light of its size.

"It's a wee bit cramped in here, too, so be careful not to hit your shins on anything. I know what you're thinking," she told him, shutting the door behind them. "This whole place could probably fit into one of your closets."

Instead of agreeing with her assessment, or being

polite about it not being so bad, Brandon took his time answering. From where he stood by the door, he could see the kitchen, the living room and the entrance to her bedroom in one small, less-than-panoramic scan.

He surprised her by laughing as he turned to her. "You should have seen my first apartment. Two of them would have fit in here—with a couple of feet to spare." He saw the disbelief in her eyes. "What, those interviews you read didn't mention that I started out as a struggling artist? Living on a shoestring—sometimes nibbling on that shoestring—are the kind of dues you're supposed to pay before you can make it as anything in the entertainment world. That includes writers.

"Besides," he went on, "I wanted to be on my own. Mother was on her fourth husband, or, more accurately, he was on her—some Russian poet she'd picked up while filming near St. Petersburg—and they needed their privacy. And I needed to hold down my breakfast. So I got this tiny hovel of an apartment and started paying my dues and suffering for my craft."

He flashed her another lethal grin—she began to realize that she would *never* accumulate any sort of immunity to them—and she could feel the charged energy that ran through his veins. "Why aren't you complaining about the clichés?" he asked. After all, he'd thrown several at her.

It never occurred to her to point out something as mundane as that. He belonged on a higher plane than having his gift for words assessed by his mother's physical therapist.

"I didn't think you wanted me to be critiquing your conversation," she admitted honestly.

"Talented and compassionate." He nodded, looking impressed. "Nice combination."

The compassionate part was easy. It was out there for the world to see, and she took pride in that, in being kind when she didn't have to be. When there was nothing in it for her but a good feeling.

But that other part—*that* made her have doubts about how sincere this man really was. "How do you know I'm talented?" she asked.

Was he hitting on her? Because of course he shouldn't be, since he was her client's son.

But, oh, he was Brandon Slade, author of ten bestselling thrillers, and gorgeous to boot. That definitely placed him in the irresistible column. And if he was hitting on her...

Life would be difficult for the next few weeks, no matter which path she wound up taking. She reminded herself that both Brandon and his mother belonged to the creative world of make-believe, and nothing they said or did could be taken seriously or to heart.

No matter how much she wanted to or how exquisitely wonderful it sounded.

"I know you're talented at what you do because I heard Mother howling in pain but she wasn't throwing you out. That means she thought you were doing her some good. Believe me, if she thought you weren't, you'd be out on your—ear," he said, changing the word he was about to use at the last moment, "in a heartbeat.

"That also," he continued, moving closer to her as if his eyesight had suddenly dimmed and he needed to be able to assess her more clearly, "puts you in a very exclusive class. Mother likes a lot of men, but there aren't too many women she likes, apart from Victoria and her own mother—and only one of them is still alive."

Brandon paused to look around her apartment for a

second time. "Actually, this is kind of charming," he pronounced.

"It's kind of cluttered," Isabelle countered, underscoring her words with a quick, dismissive shrug of her shoulders.

He regarded her thoughtfully. "Do you always do that?"

She wasn't sure what he was referring to. As far as she knew, she hadn't "done" anything, at least, not in the past couple of minutes. "Do what?"

"Deflect compliments when you get them. It's okay to accept them, you know. Doesn't make you sound vain or whatever it is that you're afraid of."

He was surprised to see, just for less than a split second, a flash of annoyance in her eyes. And it was gone so quickly, it was as if it had never even happened. But her words, uttered in no uncertain terms, testified that there had indeed been annoyance for a moment. "I'm not afraid of anything."

"And that makes you a very rare woman indeed. The brave little physical therapist," he said half to himself, as if he was considering the idea for a short story. But then he shook his head. "Gotta be a better title than that," he decided.

"Title?" she questioned.

"For a story."

Seriously? A story about a physical therapist? No, he had to be pulling her leg, she decided. She couldn't think of anything less exciting to write about, and he was known exclusively for his thrillers. Well, that and his wit. Maybe a wry sense of humor went along with that. "You're kidding, right?"

Rather than confirm or deny that he was, Brandon looked at her for a long moment. There was amusement in his eyes—and something more, something she couldn't begin to place.

"Didn't anyone warn you about writers?" he asked her.

"Warn me?" She didn't understand what he meant. "What about writers?"

"That we cannibalize everything and everyone we come in contact with, saving the best parts for the next story, keeping everything to be used in one fashion or another. Kind of like the Cheyenne did with the buffalo." He saw the blank look on Isabelle's face, so he explained his analogy. "They used absolutely every part of the buffalo they hunted, including the skin, the intestines and their—for the sake of delicacy shall we say their waste by-products? The Cheyenne used it to burn in their campfires."

Isabelle wrinkled her nose involuntarily. "Must have smelled just wonderful."

"I don't think trying to capture the scent of pleasing incense was really on their minds at the time. They were just focused on survival and feeding and clothing their families. More succinctly put, they were just trying to make it through the day."

She'd had days like that. Days when she didn't think she could make it from one end of the day to the other—and all she wanted to do was survive. And somehow, she did.

Damn it, she thought, she was letting her mind drift. Or rather, letting *him* make her mind drift.

Isabelle forced herself to focus on getting her things and getting out—as quickly as possible.

"Why don't you sit down?" she suggested, nodding toward the faux suede sofa that molded to the posterior of anyone who sat on it. "I shouldn't take too long."

He glanced at the sofa and decided he'd had enough of digging himself out of trouble for the time being. Especially since there was still the prospect of the trip back to endure.

"You don't need any help reaching for items on the top shelf in the closet?" he asked, stretching out his arm to exhibit exactly how far he could reach.

"Got it covered. I keep a step stool in the walk-in closet," she told him as she strode down the three-foot hallway to her bedroom.

Brandon grinned as he watched the way her trim hips moved in an almost seductive rhythm when she walked away. "Bet you were a Girl Scout when you were little," he called after her.

She had been, but there was no reason to confirm his suspicions. It made her seem typical and boringly predictable.

Not that she had a prayer of coming off like some mysterious femme fatale, Isabelle thought, mocking herself. She was far too wholesome for that, and hoping for anything to the contrary was just deluding herself. He was probably bored to tears already and regretting coming along. He—

Oh, God.

Too late, it hit her that she'd told him to sit down on the sofa. Which was opposite her entertainment unit. Which not only held the flat-panel TV and a number of treasured, repeatedly watched DVDs but her somewhat limited book collection.

Amid which were all of his books.

Maybe he wouldn't notice.

Mentally crossing her fingers, Isabelle quickly darted back to the living room to see what he was doing, hoping for the very thing that she'd worried about only seconds ago—that boredom had overtaken him and Brandon had fallen asleep.

Slipping silently into the living room revealed, to her disappointment, that he wasn't asleep. He wasn't even sitting. Brandon was on his feet, standing in front of the entertainment center, exploring the collection of books neatly arranged on the shelf.

Specifically, her collection of *his* books.

Rooted to the spot, she watched him for a moment, wishing for a mini-earthquake, one where the ground opened up only beneath her feet and swallowed her whole before Brandon had a chance to look up.

The ground remained frustratingly solid. So much for an earthquake.

She debated going back to the bedroom before he did look up.

And then it was too late for even that.

As if sensing her presence, Brandon glanced up from the book he was thumbing through—a well-worn copy of his third bestseller, *Speak Softly and Die*—and flashed that beguiling grin of his at her.

"You didn't tell me you were a fan. You are a fan, right?" he asked, closing the book and giving her his full attention. His expression had turned semi-serious. "I mean, you do have all my books and unless you're planning on using them to toss into the fireplace as fuel next winter—" Each of his books was easily over five hundred pages—he liked saying that he wanted to give the readers their money's worth. "—that would mean that you are, in fact, a fan."

Feeling embarrassed—although there was no reason to because, after all, it wasn't as if she was stalking the man, his mother *had* called their agency, asking for a physical therapist and according to Zoe, she just happened to be up next—Isabelle nodded her head.

"Yes, I'm a fan," she answered in a small voice which sounded as if it should be coming out of someone barely two feet tall.

In contrast, the smile on Brandon's lips would have overwhelmed a person of such small stature. It belonged, more fittingly, on the face of someone at least three times as tall.

The smile belonged, she thought, her pulse accelerating again, exactly where it was. On his, handsome, chiseled face.

"I'm flattered," he told her.

The funny thing was, despite the fact that he had veritable legions of fans, she actually believed him.

Chapter Five

Ticking off a list of necessary items in her head, Isabelle did her best to pack quickly. She focused on what she needed to take with her—the various pieces of equipment she used in her physical therapy sessions that aided her helping her clients, in this case Anastasia—and keeping them motivated.

What she was trying very hard *not* to focus on was the kneecap-melting, rapid pulse-inducing man presently wandering about her postage stamp-size living room.

She couldn't exactly put it into words as to why, but having Brandon here, in her apartment, felt almost *intimate*. She didn't need to deal with that on top of everything else. Still, she didn't want to just rush out of the apartment, conspicuously forgetting half the things she'd come back for in the first place.

Since when had she turned into this scatterbrained

creature, Isabelle silently demanded, irritated. She was the one who always prided herself on being so stable and levelheaded, so unflappable. Prided herself on always being able to know exactly what to do, at least within the parameters of her career. Zoe was forever lamenting that she was being too serious, too focused, too work-oriented.

If that was true, then where was all this fluttering pulse stuff coming from?

She was too young for a second adolescence— although she hadn't had all that much time to enjoy her first one. She could remember being this determined, this serious when she was very, very young.

It was, she supposed, all done in an effort to win her father's approval. Her father had been a neurosurgeon, well-known in his circles, and her mother had been high up on the board of Swan Laboratories. Both had expected great things from their daughters. As far as each of them was concerned, "physical therapist" did not come under the heading of "great things."

Because Zoe ran the company, her parents saw some merit in her career, but as for Isabelle, well, she was "little better than a glorified masseuse." At least, that was the way her father had put it. There'd been a disdainful expression on his patrician face at the time.

That had been shortly before her entire world had fallen apart. Before she'd discovered that her father was cheating on her mother. And before learning that this was only the latest "indiscretion" in a very long list of indiscretions.

Finding out that the man who'd always demanded nothing but the best from her apparently didn't believe he needed to measure up to the same standards himself had taken a huge toll on her. She'd never thought her parents had a loving relationship, but she'd thought it was built on mutual respect and trust. Discovering she was wrong had nearly crushed her. It had made her look to her career for satisfaction rather than to any kind of a relationship.

The breakup of her parents' marriage had accomplished one more thing. Never close to her mother and now estranged from her father, Isabelle had found herself free to make whatever she wanted of her life. She chose to follow the path she'd originally set out for herself.

That path, she now silently emphasized as she quickly tucked a few essentials into the overnight case lying opened on her queen-size bed, did *not* include being some starry-eyed fanatical "groupie" who lost the ability to think beyond three-word sentences just because a handsome specimen of manhood like Brandon Slade was sitting in her living room.

Waiting for her.

Waiting for his mother's physical therapist, Isabelle tersely corrected herself. It wasn't as if he actually saw her as a *woman*. She was just a genderless being whose assignment was to get his mother up, walking and then, hopefully, dancing within a finite amount of time.

She'd always liked challenges, Isabelle reminded herself, and this certainly promised to be one.

Stuffing her most frequently used reference manual on top of the rest of her things, she pushed down hard and struggled with the case's zipper, slowly managing to drag it up and around the three sides of her navy blue suitcase. Swinging the suitcase off the bed, she proceeded out into the living room, listing ever so slightly to one side. The suitcase proved to be heavier than she'd anticipated.

Brandon looked up the moment she entered the room,

putting the book he'd been paging through back into its place on the shelf.

"Here, let me," he offered, quickly cutting the distance between them and slipping his hand over hers in order to take possession of the suitcase handle.

Isabelle swallowed in an attempt to moisten a mouth that had gone powder dry. She could have sworn an intense zap of electricity shot between them. At least, it crackled on her end and jolted her right down to her suddenly curled toes.

"That's okay," she demurred, still holding on to the handle. "It's not heavy."

The hell it wasn't, he thought. Brandon continued to keep his hand on top of hers, waiting for her to give up the pretense and surrender the suitcase.

When she didn't, he asked, "Am I going to have to wrestle you for it?" Amusement curved the corners of his mouth as his eyes captured hers.

Breathe, damn it. Breathe! Isabelle ordered herself. *What is the matter with you? He's just a man. Magnificent, maybe, but still just a man. You know all the body parts. You had to name them on one of your final exams, remember? Get a grip, for heaven's sake, will you?* She hoped against hope that she wasn't turning a bright shade of pink before Brandon's magnificent blue eyes. Her skin certainly felt hot enough.

Until this very moment, she'd thought that blushing in such circumstances was just a myth, experienced by socially repressed women of the early last century, not by an educated, capable and independent woman of the twenty-first century.

And yet, here she was, feeling heat creeping up the sides of her neck, slipping over her cheeks and threatening to turn the color of her skin into the same shade as cotton candy.

That'll impress him.

"No," she heard herself saying as she slipped her hand out from beneath his and gave up her claim to possession of the handle. "No need to wrestle me." Not that the idea didn't have very real, appealing possibilities, she added silently.

The next moment, she tamped down her wayward thoughts and focused strictly on getting back to her patient. It wasn't easy when the man seemed to fill up every corner of the apartment with his presence.

And his smile.

Leading the way, Isabelle opened the door, then paused to look over her shoulder for a moment.

Standing beside her, Brandon followed her line of vision. And saw nothing amiss. "Forget something?" he asked.

"Just going over a mental checklist to make sure I didn't," she confessed.

She'd taught herself to do the mental checklist every time she left the apartment after once accidentally leaving the air-conditioning on high instead of turning it off. It had run almost continuously for thirteen hours, much to the joy of the electric company and the sadness of her checking account when it had come time to pay that month's bill.

Turning back toward the door, she saw the smile that entered his eyes. "What?"

"I don't think I've ever met anyone as organized as you before—myself included," he told her. After growing up with his mother and the eccentric people who populated both Anastasia's world and his own, someone like Isabelle was a breath of fresh air.

His voice gave her no clue if he was compliment-
ing her—or mocking her. Everything he said always
sounded so upbeat and cheerful.

"Is that a good thing or a bad thing?" she heard herself asking.

"A good thing. Definitely a good thing," he assured
her as they walked to her car. The moment they reached
it, a look of dread mingled with resignation came into
his eyes. "I'd almost forgotten about this," he murmured,
sounding far from happy.

Was it his imagination, or had the space gotten even
smaller?

Isabelle unlocked the car's trunk, and he deposited
her overnight bag into it. Though it was a small case,
the trunk seemed even smaller and the suitcase took up
most of the available space.

She did her best to sound encouraging. "Well, on
the positive side, it's not that long a trip," she reminded
him.

But it was.

Traffic, rarely free-flowing no matter what time of
day or night travel occurred, became utterly snarled as
several lanes were closed down due to an unfortunate
collision between a truck associated with a nationally
known supermarket chain and a silver SUV so new it
didn't even have its official DMV license plates in place
yet. The latter vehicle had gone flying on impact and
was currently on its back like some battered, disabled
turtle.

Miraculously, the three passengers in the SUV had
not only survived the accident, but once the fire department had managed to cut them out of the inverted
vehicle, they had emerged with only a minimum of cuts
and scratches.

The traffic, however, did not fare nearly as well, threatening to keep everyone in both directions glued in their positions with the hope of only succeeding to travel a couple of inches forward every few minutes—if even that much.

Slanting a glance toward Brandon, Isabelle asked, "How are you doing?"

More than forty-five minutes had passed, and they had managed to go less than half a mile. At this rate, they'd be back at his house by evening—and he would have to be retaught how to walk.

"Well," Brandon confessed, "if we wind up stuck like this much longer, by the time we *do* get home, I'm going to need the jaws of life to cut me out of here." He looked down at the crammed space and the way his legs were tucked in. His knees were flat up against what passed for a glove compartment. "I think my legs are going numb. I know I don't feel my toes anymore."

It was all her fault. She should have never let him fold himself up into her little car like this. She was fine with it the way it was, but, without her high heels on, she was a whole foot shorter than he was.

"I feel just awful," she told him.

Brandon tried to shrug away her assessment and discovered that he didn't have enough room to complete the movement. His right shoulder hit the inside of the passenger door.

"Not your fault," he told her, absolving her of any blame.

Isabelle didn't see it that way. Had she not agreed to his coming along—secretly *thrilled* at the very idea of spending time alone with him in any setting—he wouldn't be currently playing the part of an oversize fish stuffed into a sardine can.

By nature, even if she hadn't become a physical therapist, Isabelle had a calling to be a caregiver. Someone who felt it was her assigned mission in life to fix each and every problem to the very best of her ability. Given that, and her guilt, she had a very strong need to do something to remedy Brandon's unacceptable situation.

Working her lower lip between her teeth, she cast about for a way to ease Brandon's discomfort. The only way that was remotely possible was to get the man out of her tiny car.

But he couldn't very well walk home from here—

Searching the area, she suddenly *saw* it, saw the way things were set up. Although cars were now restricted to a single lane going in either direction, there was the remnant of a shoulder available to her on the right side. It wasn't anything an SUV could travel, but her vehicle was the size of a Smart Car with a gland condition.

In two short moments, she made up her mind. Bracing herself, she suddenly darted into the space on the right. Once there, she immediately began maneuvering her way down toward the junction up ahead where, according to the information on her GPS, the traffic let up, the speed picked up to that of regular freeway travel and the entire way from there to his house was, for the most part, unobstructed.

Surprised at the sudden shift onto the sidewalk and the fact that she was now driving in the defensive manner of an Indianapolis 500 racer, Brandon eyed her uncertainly. She'd just broken the law—or bent it in several places at the very least.

They were picking up more speed, passing the other cars with absolutely no trouble. He could swear envious looks were being shot in their direction.

"What are you doing?" he asked.

She would have thought that would have been rather obvious. "Getting you home before you lose the ability to walk," she answered simply.

He didn't want her getting into trouble on his account.

"If a policeman sees you, you're liable to get one hell of a large fine," he warned. Not that he would allow Isabelle to pay it, he added silently. She could hardly afford it, while he, on the other hand, would hardly notice it.

She'd been very alert, searching for any sign of a police vehicle. She hadn't seen any of Newport Beach's finest in the vicinity.

"I'll play the odds," she told him.

So far, her vigilance had worked, and the odds had remained in her favor. She'd never gotten a ticket, and although she was far from being a speed demon, she wasn't exactly a timid saint on the road, either.

Despite his growing physical discomfort, Brandon took a scrutinizing second look at this young woman who was traveling up the shoulder of the road as if it was the most natural thing to do.

"You know, until just now, I thought you were a sweet girl-next-door type. But there's a lot more to you than first meets the eye, isn't there? You, Isabelle Sinclair, are a very complicated woman," he concluded.

She spared just the most fleeting of glances in his direction. The smile she saw on his face went directly to her gut. It made risking a ticket utterly worthwhile. The addition of a compliment just put the whole thing over the top.

She got him home far faster than he thought possible. At the end of the trip, he came to the conclusion that his mother's little physical therapist drove like a pro. A racing pro. He wondered if it came naturally by way of genes, or was it just something she did by rising to the occasion?

The next moment, as he opened the door on his side and tried to get out, all other thoughts vacated his head. There was nothing to focus on *except* getting out of the car.

Or not getting out of the car, as the case was turning out.

"How are they?" Isabelle asked, concerned.

The second she'd pulled up into the driveway and set the parking brake, she'd leaped out of the vehicle and quickly rounded the nonexistent hood to come to his side. He'd already opened the passenger door. Isabelle opened it wider.

And then she remained standing there, looking at Brandon's lower half as he attempted, unsuccessfully, to unfold himself and get out. It became painfully obvious that he was having difficulties after his second attempt failed.

"Numb," he answered honestly. "But I think there's hope."

Brandon had always subscribed to the glass half-full school of thought. Nothing could be gained by anticipating the worst. If it was meant to happen, it would happen. No sense in ushering it in prematurely and giving it a seat at the table.

Bracing one hand on the inside of the passenger door, the other against the headrest, Brandon finally managed to attain his freedom from the imprisoning sports car. Once out, he did his best to push himself up into a standing position. It was far from easy. His legs really had gone numb, and now there was that incredibly annoying feeling of a myriad of ants sashaying back and forth along the backs of his thighs and calves.

He still didn't feel his feet.

Standing, although a bit unsteadily, he made eye contact with Isabelle. "But the prognosis is good," he said just before he took a step forward.

The next moment, his right knee buckled, and he found himself sinking. He would have gone down all the way had Isabelle not instinctively sprang into action. She instantly placed her body in the way, angling her shoulder so that it was solidly beneath his. She caught the full brunt of his weight.

For a second, Isabelle sank down a little, her knees temporarily weakened because of the added weight. But then, with one arm wrapped firmly around his midsection, and relying on sheer determination—and the exercises she did religiously whenever she found the time—she managed to hold Brandon in place.

Brandon was clearly surprised. She weighed far less than he did. How, then, did she manage to support his weight and not buckle under? She really was rather an amazing woman, he thought as admiration flooded through him.

"You weren't kidding, were you? You really are strong, especially for such a little thing," he couldn't help commenting.

Had her shoulders been free, she would have shrugged off the compliment. "It's all in the technique," she told him. Concerned about the condition of his legs, she added, "We'll just stand here for a while until you feel up to walking inside."

"Until then I guess we could practice singing some old beer drinking songs," he deadpanned, leaning into her.

She stared, confused. He looked so serious, she couldn't tell if he was kidding or not. "What?"

"Just a joke," he assured her. "With my arm draped like that over your shoulders, it reminded me of my slightly beer-hazy days in college where the reward for getting through a week of studies was to go to the local pub, swap stories and drink. The drinks got progressively taller, the stories got progressively shorter and then, in the end, we'd all stumble back to the dorms, the less plastered holding up the more plastered."

At the time, it had seemed like the fun thing to do. Now, looking back, he wondered why he'd wasted the time and the money. He hoped to God that Victoria would prove to be more mature than he had been when it was her turn to go to college.

Hell, he thought, she was more mature *now* than he had been then.

"Sounds like a lovely time," Isabelle commented dryly.

"It was then. In hindsight, though, maybe not so much." He looked at her. He'd done more than his share of talking. It was time to find out something about her. "What was your college experience like?"

"Lots of studying. No stories. No beer."

She felt almost envious of Brandon's experiences because she'd had none to speak of, no fond memories to look back on. There had been just goals to reach and parents to impress. Succeeding in the former didn't really make up for failing in the latter.

"Sounds like something I'm hoping Victoria experiences," he told her honestly. And then, the next moment, he interrupted himself as his face lit up. "Wait, I think I feel something," he announced. Looking down at his feet, he proclaimed with a grin. "Yes, definitely something. I feel my feet."

Very slowly, like a man testing the waters, Brandon removed his arm from her shoulders.

His weight gone, Isabelle instantly straightened up. She did her damnedest not to look as if she even noticed the contact between them was terminated. Or that she missed it.

Chapter Six

"Can't you do anything to speed this up?" Anastasia asked impatiently.

It was several days later. Isabelle and her less-than-patient patient were in the room that Brandon had equipped to serve as his private indoor gym. Open and airy, with a massage table on one side and mirrors running along the length of two of the walls, reflecting a number of different exercise machines, it was the perfect location for Anastasia's therapy, Isabelle thought. The mirrored walls would allow the actress to see for herself what she was doing wrong—and improve upon what she was doing right.

At the moment, the movie icon felt it was a great deal of the former and not nearly enough of the latter.

"You're doing very well," Isabelle assured her in the calm, upbeat voice that was her stock-in-trade when she worked with restless clients.

"Are you sure this is how this therapy stuff is supposed to go?" the woman questioned with more than a touch of frustration in her voice. "I thought I'd be lying on a table, having you knead the muscles around the affected area to get them back into shape."

"That's not therapy, that's a massage," Isabelle pointed out, her smile never leaving her lips. "Speaking of which, let's get you up on the table," she directed.

"For a massage?" Anastasia asked, brightening.

"No, to rotate the leg that was operated on, see if we can't stretch those muscles of yours a little," Isabelle told her.

Because she didn't want the actress pulling anything, Isabelle discreetly moved a single-step step stool into place, getting Anastasia to use that in order to help her get on the table.

With effort, Anastasia lowered herself onto the table, then looked at her.

"Okay, now what?"

"Now, you lie down," Isabelle said, gently taking hold of the woman's leg and lifting it upward, "and we do this."

Anastasia's eyes widened, unprepared for the salvo of pain that shot through her. The anguished cry escaped the woman's lips before she could think to stop it—not that she would have. "Aren't you supposed to make a wish first before snapping the bone?"

"That's only with a wishbone and there'll be no bone snapping today," Isabelle promised. "Just a couple more times," she coaxed, rotating the leg even more slowly. "You're doing fine."

"*That* is a matter of opinion," Anastasia grumbled.

Unfazed, Isabelle continued smiling and slowly rotating the woman's leg from side to side to encompass what she felt were its essential limits for now. "Don't worry, this'll seem like nothing to you soon."

Anastasia wanted something more definite than that. "When?" she demanded.

"When your body gets a little stronger." Stopping, Isabelle lowered the woman's leg and leaned back. They both relaxed. "This is a slow process, Anastasia, and you're already making more progress than most patients in your age bracket."

Somewhat pleased, Anastasia still saw fit to challenge her. "Is that your polite way of saying that I'm old?"

"No, that's my way of using the data that's been compiled about the response rate of various different groups of people as a reference point. This way, as your physical therapist, I know more or less what to expect by way of normal progress—and what to shoot for."

Anastasia looked unconvinced. She sniffed slightly. "That's very diplomatic."

Isabelle wasn't about to be baited. Her father used to do that, trying to trap her into admissions she had no desire of making. He felt it was his way of showing off his superiority. She'd learned how to make the most of evasive maneuvers.

"It's just the truth. Now, do you want to rest or continue a little longer?"

"I want to rest," Anastasia declared. But even as she said so, the actress propped herself up on her elbows, braced for anything. "But I'll continue a little longer." And then she glanced toward the doorway and raised her voice. "Preferably without an audience."

Now *there* was something she thought she'd never hear from the actress, Isabelle thought as she turned around to see who the woman was talking to.

Brandon.

Three days into her stay and the sight of the handsome author still caused her heart to flutter like a butterfly caught in an updraft.

How long was it going to take for her to get used to having him pop up like that? She had a feeling she knew the answer to that, and it was *not* one that worked in her favor.

"Don't worry, I'm not staying," Brandon told his mother as he popped into the room. He nodded a greeting coupled with a smile at Isabelle before shifting back to his mother. "Just wanted to tell you that I'll be out for a while. Do you need anything before I go? Pillows fluffed, foot massaged, a cup of coffee...?" he teased, his voice trailing off.

"I'm sure Isabelle will indulge me if I find I want something. Where are you off to?" Anastasia suddenly narrowed her eyes as a possible answer occurred to her. "You're not seeing that dreadful Wanda person again, are you?"

"No, I'm not," Brandon replied patiently. "And go easy on her. She was just a reporter, doing an interview. My last book is being reissued in paperback next week, remember? Publicity never hurts, no matter how big you think you are."

Isabelle had read that interview by Wanda Miller. Brandon had come off very well, but then, he always did. It was to his credit that he gave himself no airs, did not think of himself as being too big to fail. He made it a point to always cooperate with the press, and they apparently loved him for it.

Anastasia seemed to stop listening halfway through her son's reply. Instead, she shook her head, a look of incredulousness entering her famous eyes. "Just a reporter—ha! How is it you got to be thirty-two years old and still have no clue about women?"

For a fleeting moment, his eyes connected with Isabelle's, and then he shifted to his mother. "I guess that some mysteries are just meant to remain that way."

The actress's sigh was deep and despairing. "You need a keeper," Anastasia pronounced.

Brandon grinned good-naturedly. He took no offense. He was used to his mother's broad strokes, whether with a brush on a canvas, or verbally. "I have you and Victoria—what more do I need?"

Anastasia gave a gentle snort, as if withdrawing from the field of battle for the moment. "You still haven't said where you're going," his mother reminded him.

"No, I didn't," he agreed just before he began to walk out of the gym.

"Brandon."

Only Anastasia Del Vecchio could have infused so many emotions and nuances into the two syllables of his name, Isabelle thought, utterly impressed. The single utterance spoke volumes without saying any more than just his name.

Brandon paused in the doorway. "I'm scouting out locations for my next book," he told her.

By nature Brandon was a very visual person. He found that he needed to see something, to be part of it, before he could adequately describe it and hope to do it justice. Once it was there, in his memory banks, he could take off from that point and weave a location of his own. But he needed a starting point.

"I've always been partial to the area near Laguna Beach," his mother told him. "It reminds me of this little hotel on the Riviera where your father and I honeymooned. Before I discovered he was a scoundrel."

She heaved a heartfelt sigh. And then, as if she'd suddenly been struck with this most original thought, she suggested, "Why don't you have Isabelle go with you? She can be your sounding board."

"I don't need a sounding board for a location, Mother," he told her patiently, then reconsidered his words. "But I could use the company." He turned toward Isabelle. "How about it? Are you up for a little aimless driving?"

If he was being honest with himself, he wasn't just in search of a location. He was looking for a plot to go with that location and really hoped that the one—when he found something that moved him—would wind up triggering the other.

It wouldn't be the first time.

Just what was happening here? Confused, Isabelle looked at the older woman. "I thought you said you wanted to push on."

Anastasia started to get down from the table, then hesitated, trying to decide which foot to put down first, the one that belonged to her brand-new hip, or the one where it was business as usual. After a beat, she held off on her decision.

"I changed my mind," Anastasia announced with a touch of haughtiness. Softening, she addressed the puzzled look on Isabelle's face. "It's what I do."

"Yes, I know. Oh, so well," Brandon couldn't resist adding.

"That'll be enough out of you," his mother declared with an air of finality. She left no room for even the slightest argument. That done, the woman turned her attention to her physical therapist.

"Go, get some fresh air. Renew your 'juices,' or whatever it is that you call them," Anastasia ordered, waving her hand toward the doorway. "You're of no use to me if you're exhausted when we start out."

Isabelle wasn't sure what the actress was talking about. She had certainly never approached their sessions together with anything but bright enthusiasm and energy. It was one of her work principles to always be upbeat and positive with a client and to never allow them to become discouraged or, worse, to allow herself to behave in a discouraged manner around them. She was getting paid to help, not to whine.

"Brandon," she called, summoning him as she held out her hand in a gesture that was nothing short of regal. "Be a good boy and help your mother off the table."

"Now there's a line I hope no one ever overhears," he quipped to Isabelle. Coming to his mother's side with sure, strong hands, he bracketed her body on either side. The next moment, he was scooping her off the tale as if Anastasia weighed perhaps fifty pounds.

Upright and on her feet again, Anastasia slowly released her grip on the back of Brandon's neck. "Thank you, dear. Now run along, both of you. I have some lines to run."

He looked at her suspiciously. His mother was a notoriously social creature who rarely did anything alone. "By yourself?"

"No," Victoria said, coming into the room to see if her grandmother was ready yet. "Gemma asked me to cue her."

Brandon pretended not to care for the idea. "You're just trying to brainwash my very levelheaded daughter and secretly turn her into an actress wannabe. Isn't one in the family enough?"

Anastasia merely shook her head, as if pitying someone who was so suspicious. The truth was, if her granddaughter wanted to follow in her footsteps, she would have happily moved heaven and earth to make it happen.

"I haven't the vaguest idea what you're babbling about, dear," she told Brandon. "I have always been *more* than enough for my audiences and Victoria's just helping me out by cuing me. Now go, shoo. You're distracting me. Both of you."

Using the hand-carved cane that Brandon had gifted her with just before she came home from the hospital, Anastasia took small baby steps toward her granddaughter. Draping one arm a bit more heavily than she would have liked to over the girl's slender, sturdy shoulders she asked, "Ready to run through those lines with me?"

Victoria had a smile that lit up a room. Anastasia liked to say the girl got it from her. "Absolutely, Gemma."

"Well, I'm set for the afternoon," Anastasia pronounced. She looked at her son and Isabelle. "Now, go, both of you." As they began to leave, Anastasia raised her voice and called out after Brandon, "Maybe she can help you with your writer's block."

Stunned, Isabelle looked at him. This was something new. Brandon Slade was regarded as exceedingly prolific and never at a loss for either ideas or words. "You have writer's block?"

"I do *not* have writer's block." The strongly voiced denial was aimed at his mother, not Isabelle. His tone softened as he walked out of the gym and addressed her. "It just hasn't come all together for me yet," he allowed evasively. "Doesn't mean that it won't," he added quickly.

Isabelle nodded. There was no reason to believe that it wouldn't. "And you're hoping if you see the right locale, the story will start falling into place for you."

"Exactly." There was gratitude in Brandon's eyes when he looked at her just as they reached the front door. "You understand."

"I do a lot of that in my line of work. Understanding," she clarified when he continued regarding her, looking just the slightest bit baffled. "I understand what they're going through. I understand the frustration when their progress isn't going as fast as they would like it to. And I understand why they resort to procrastination when they should be pushing forward." He opened the front door, waiting for her to walk out first. But she remained standing where she was. "Listen, you don't need me to tag along. I understand that you agreed just to humor your mother—"

"Then maybe you're not as 'understanding' as you think," he contradicted. "I really would like the company," he assured her, adding, "and you could give me another take on the location."

She doubted he needed anyone else's input. At least, not hers. "Isn't writing really the ultimate intimate experience? You dig into yourself to get the story, the emotions, the specific characteristics of your people—"

"All true," he agreed. But she was overlooking something. "The bottom line is that I do it to entertain my readers and to bring in a few thousand more. In other words, the general public." Very gently, he ushered her out the door and closed it behind him. "You could be my public—unless you have something else to do," he interjected. It occurred to him that he just might have taken too much for granted by assuming Isabelle would be willing to drop everything to hop into the car with him and take off.

Isabelle didn't answer immediately. Instead, she appeared to seriously consider the matter. Putting her hands out as if she were actually weighing two things, she lifted first her right hand, then her left, murmuring under her breath in what was a stage whisper, "Hmm, doing my laundry, scouting out a location for a new Brandon Slade thriller. Hard call, but I think the scouting thing has a slight edge." Dropping her hands, her eyes crinkled as she laughed. "Let's go."

For the first time, he noticed that Isabelle had a dimple in the corner of her mouth. It was only on the right, and it was damn near delectable, Brandon caught himself thinking.

Trying not to dwell on that, or the thoughts about her mouth it brought with it, he led Isabelle toward the six-car garage.

The temperature-controlled enclosure currently housed only three vehicles, his two rather expensive cars and the vintage Mercedes that his mother favored.

He'd had the latter brought over in case his mother felt like going for a drive as part of her recovery program. He judged that they were at least two weeks away from her getting behind the wheel at this point.

The rest of the garage, Isabelle noted as they entered, was devoted to an entertainment center, a pool table and all the possible accessories belonging to a first-class gaming area, including a fully-stocked refrigerator.

"You throw a lot of parties here?" she asked, looking around in awe.

"A few," he conceded. "After I finish working on a book, I like to touch base with my friends. Actually, a lot of them are also my mother's friends," he admitted. He liked keeping in touch with that eccentric crowd. There were many fond memories associated with them. "I was like their mascot when I was growing up. Writing can be a very lonely experience and I like balancing it out by socializing with people when I can. Besides, talking to people—" and by this he included anyone who crossed his path "—always gives me fresh ideas."

"Right, you cannibalize everyone," she said, remembering what he'd told her the other day.

"I've got to find a better word for it," he decided, bringing her over to his SUV.

Because it was a customized white SUV, there was a regal quality to it that made it look like more than just a fun car.

Opening the passenger door for her, Brandon waited until Isabelle got in. Then he closed it again before rounding the hood and getting into the driver's side.

"Notice the leg room," he couldn't resist pointing out.

"I notice it," she answered, then looked up at him. "Another six inches and I could probably go bowling in it."

He laughed as he put his key in the ignition. "Wise guy."

She smiled to herself as Brandon pressed the remote control attached to the sun visor that was above his side of the windshield. Directly behind them the garage door silently slid upward until, tucked away, it seemed to completely disappear from view. The garage was instantly bright with sunshine.

"Do you have to be back any particular time?" he asked her.

She hadn't gotten around to giving Anastasia the schedules she'd drawn up, so she felt she could be forgiven a small white lie, uttered in hopes of extending her time with him a little longer.

"Nothing specific," Isabelle answered. "Just to exercise your mother again."

"Perfect," he pronounced with an affirming nod. "That means the afternoon is completely wide open. She's running lines with Victoria, and whenever she does that, Mother gets completely consumed by the character she's learning to inhabit. Knowing her, she won't be up for air for hours."

Isabelle thought of Victoria. The girl might behave maturely, acting years older than what was written on her birth certificate, but at bottom, she was still a twelve-year-old.

"Is your daughter up to that? Running lines with her grandmother for hours?" It seemed like a lot to ask of the girl.

"She's up to it all right." There was no small amount of pride in Brandon's voice as he added, "Victoria's a very exceptional girl."

Being exceptional obviously ran in the family, Isabelle couldn't help thinking as she slanted a covert glance at Victoria's father.

The next moment, the SUV picked up speed, and they were off.

As was, Isabelle noted, her pulse. Again.

Chapter Seven

The road leading to Laguna Beach ran through various beach communities that dotted the coast. Brandon drove along unhurried, lightly skimming around Pacific Coast Highway's twists and turns, as comfortable as a man visiting old friends to seek out their advice.

Except that it was different this time.

Different because this time, he had someone with him. Someone he could talk to. Someone he could, if need be, bounce half-formed ideas off of.

With songs from a bygone era softly playing in the background on the oldies station he had preset on his radio, Brandon did his best to focus, to home in on some kind of a kernel of thought that would start the process finally moving in the right direction for him.

He refused to believe that, after ten well-received bestsellers and a new one about to hit the shelves in a couple of weeks, that he was suddenly dry. Refused to entertain the thought that his best work was now behind him.

Still, he had to admit that he was more focused on the young woman in the passenger seat next to him than he was on anything he could put down on the page.

Was it her fault he couldn't think—or had he brought her along to give himself an excuse for not thinking?

At this point, he wasn't sure. It was a "chicken or egg" sort of question.

Thinking it might help seed the barren terrain that was his ordinarily fruitful mind, Brandon decided to get a conversation rolling.

Turning down the radio, he asked Isabelle, "What made you become a physical therapist?"

The question came out of the blue, catching Isabelle off guard. It took her a second to realize Brandon was talking to her. He'd been quiet since they'd turned onto Pacific Coast Highway, and she just assumed that he was plotting a scene in his head or something along those lines. She hadn't wanted to interrupt him.

But now that he'd addressed her, she felt she was free to talk to him. She started by answering his question. "Well, my sister would tell you it's because I like to order people around and make them do what I tell them, but the truth is simpler than that. I like helping people. I have an aptitude for it. I can motivate people, get them fired up to try again instead of giving up. Having a small part in their healing makes me feel good," she told him honestly.

"You're a very persuasive woman." Brandon wasn't trying to flatter her. There weren't many people who could hold their own with his mother. The fact that she could said a great deal about her strength of character, and that impressed him.

She moved her shoulders in a vague shrug, dismissing his assessment. "No, not really, but for some reason, I can tap into their innermost feelings. I can find that hidden spark that'll make them try again and again until they conquer that particular hurdle and move on to the next one."

Brandon nodded, understanding. "You mean like with my mother."

Anastasia Del Vecchio was opinionated and stubborn, but the woman, despite her complaints, *really* wanted to get back to her former self. That gave her something to work with, Isabelle thought.

"Your mother's one of the easier cases," she told him. When he responded to that with a laugh, she explained. "No, really. She wants to be pushed. I think if I played it strictly the way she makes it 'appear' that she wants it—stopping for a break every few minutes and taking the easy way out—your mother would complain even louder—and really mean it. She'd probably demand to know why I was giving up on her. For her, it's all part of the process. She *wants* me to ride roughshod over her so she can grumble and complain—and get back to her old self. You know, for a woman her age, your mother's in fantastic shape."

Amused, Brandon laughed softly under his breath. "You know, if you value your life, I wouldn't mention that part about 'a woman her age' anywhere that she can overhear you. My mother's age is a secret guarded only a little less zealously than security at the White House. How do you know how old she is, anyway?" he asked. Even he wasn't a hundred percent certain that he had the right year.

"I've been a fan of your mother's ever since I can

remember," she told him. "Back then, she didn't care if people knew what year she was born."

Shaking his head, he laughed. "Now there you're wrong. Anastasia Del Vecchio *always* cared about keeping her age off the record. My mother wanted to be thought of as 'timeless' and 'eternally young.' To be honest," Brandon went on to admit, "*I'm* not even sure if *I* know how old she is."

She studied his profile for a moment. "Doesn't that bother you?" She knew that it would drive her absolutely crazy not to know.

"Not really." Brandon shrugged away the question. "It's just part of what makes her Anastasia Del Vecchio. She's quicksilver. Mercurial. Someone who can't be pinned down." He glanced over to his right. They traveled along another stretch of beach, passing an RV camping area. In direct contrast to the RVs, some of Laguna's most expensive homes were nested on his left. "What matters more to me than any chronological number is that when I really needed her, she was there— without my having to actually say a word to her."

"When you found yourself suddenly being a single father."

The road ahead was empty. Brandon allowed himself a moment to glance at her. "So you know about that, too." It was obviously not a question, but neither was it an accusation.

Still, she blushed just a little at having verbally intruded into a private matter. "You were always an extension of your mother's life, so bits and pieces of yours made it into stories that were written about her. And then you wrote your first thriller and became famous in your own right. Interviews followed..."

Her voice trailed off as she realized that might have

sounded a tad obsessive to him. She hadn't been keeping tabs on him, she was just mildly interested in her favorite author's life. And she had *always* been interested in Anastasia Del Vecchio. It was still difficult for her to grasp that she was giving the legendary star physical therapy and living within shouting distance of the woman.

Isabelle pressed her lips together. There were so many questions popping into her mind, things she wanted to know about the man, the writer, firsthand. "Mind if I ask you something?"

They were coming to a sharp turn. He kept his eyes on the road. "Go ahead."

Since he'd asked her about her work, she thought that allowed her to ask him a question about his. "Did you always want to be a writer?"

There'd been a few other choices: cowboy, astronaut, but those had faded by the time he was nine. The only serious career he'd ever considered was the one he had now.

"Well, seeing the world I was part of, creating fantasy just came naturally to me. I was always making up stories in my head, exciting stories—or so I thought," he qualified with a self-deprecating grin. "Stories where I was the hero, saving the girl, and coincidentally, saving the world as well. Modest little stories," he added with a soft laugh. "When it came time to earn a living, there was nothing else I wanted to be except a writer. The idea excited me. Fortunately for me, I had gotten better at making up stories."

Part of his skill had been honed to near perfection in the process of making up alibis for why his assignments weren't in on time, or why he'd missed attending one class or another.

There'd been a teacher, a dour looking professor with thick gray hair and an even thicker Scottish brogue, who'd told him that he might be better off putting his fertile mind to some sort of productive use that didn't involve fabricating elaborate excuses. After a bit, he'd decided to take the professor's words to heart and, as people liked to say, the rest was history.

They'd entered Laguna Beach proper, with its tiny, artsy shops, a couple of minutes ago. Brandon hadn't even noticed. He took a second to orient himself. A pinch in his gut told him what time it was.

"Are you hungry?" Brandon asked.

The question had come out of left field. She glanced at her watch and realized that they had been driving around for almost an hour. If anything, she would have assumed he'd turn around to go back, not suggest staying out longer.

Maybe he *really* didn't want to go back and stare at his blank computer screen, she thought. If that was the case, she was happy to play along and give him an excuse. Besides, she really *was* hungry. "Why, is my stomach growling?"

"No, but I just realized we're coming up on The Enchanted Cottage, and I don't know about you, but I left without having any lunch."

She hadn't eaten lunch, either, and breakfast was a blur. But she was more interested right now in the name he'd just casually dropped. "The Enchanted Cottage?" she repeated. "Isn't that an old movie with Robert Young and Dorothy McGuire?"

They were at a light, and he took the opportunity to stare at her in wonder. "I've never met anyone else who'd ever heard of the movie. Did you even *have* a childhood?" he asked.

"Yes, and that was it, watching old movies." Getting lost in stories that were larger than life had helped her deal with a cold upbringing.

"Well, I'm impressed," he freely admitted. "So, are you hungry?"

She could literally *feel* her stomach tightening in both protest and anticipation. She nodded. "I could eat, yes."

That was all he wanted to hear. Brandon grinned. "Great."

As it turned out, the restaurant, which looked like a quaint cottage, was just up ahead, nestled on the corner to his left at the next traffic light. It was timed to turn red as he approached and then took its own sweet time turning green again, despite the fact that there was no through traffic to merit the long wait.

The moment it turned green, Brandon drove down the side street and searched for a place to park. Half a block later, he found it. He carefully slipped his vehicle between a truck and a sports car with an ease she couldn't help admiring.

"You parallel park." There was no missing the note of awe in her voice. She was lucky to manage head-in parking. Wedging a vehicle between two tight places was definitely *not* one of her favorite activities. She was fairly certain that she couldn't do it.

"I also know all the stanzas to 'The Star Spangled Banner,'" Brandon quipped as he pulled up the emergency brake and turned off the ignition.

"A man with endless talents," Isabelle remarked with only partially feigned admiration.

Getting out of the vehicle, he laughed. "I guess that accurately sums me up."

The next moment, the laugh faded as he quickly

jumped into action. Grabbing Isabelle by the shoulder, he yanked her back, away from the street.

Caught off guard, she stumbled, and her body slammed into his. All their parts fitted together splendidly, leaving no space for even a glimmer of daylight.

The reason for the sudden action was to prevent Isabelle from being hit by a careening, all-but-out-of-control sports car whose driver had obviously taken to celebrating heavily a little early in the day. The sound of tires screeching and wailing as the driver narrowly avoided smashing into several parked cars on the next block vaguely registered along the outer perimeter of her mind.

What registered in the foreground was heat.

Lots and lots of heat.

None of which was emanating from the beach a mere block away as the crow flew. It was being created from the very firm, very enticing contact of their two bodies momentarily sealed against one another in the most natural, albeit the most sensually provocative, of ways.

Was that his heart beating like a wild drum, or hers? At this point, she couldn't tell. She only knew that she was in very real danger of melting as the feeling of excitement all but roared through her veins like a charging rhino.

"Sorry," Brandon murmured, looking down into her eyes, making no effort to pull away.

"Nothing to be sorry about," she replied, the words leaving her mouth in what felt like slow motion, in direct contrast to the wild throbbing of her pulse. It beat so hard, she thought it would shatter her wrists. "You just saved me from being flattened," she managed to conclude. She congratulated herself on not sounding too breathless.

Shaking himself free of the spell that she'd woven around him, he pretended to look up and down the rurallike street.

"Never a cop around when you need one," he complained under his breath.

She was just now coming to grips with what *could* have happened. "Good thing you were here."

His eyes skimmed over her body, none the worse for wear, he decided. "Yeah. Good thing," he parroted.

God, but the conversation was inane. It had to be brought up two notches before it could even qualify as "lame."

He could do so much better on paper, Brandon told himself. *Had* done so much better in real life. But that was when his brain was functioning, capable of forming complete sentences. Right now, all he could think of was that he wanted to kiss this woman. Wanted to kiss her in the very worst possible way. Kiss her for a very long time.

But she was his mother's physical therapist, and somehow, kissing her just didn't seem right.

The next moment, he rebelled at the restriction. The hell with right.

The last phrase echoed in his head as he cupped the sides of Isabelle's face with his hands. By turns he saw the surprise, the wonder and then the surrender in her eyes. She tilted her head back ever so slightly.

The silent invitation was clear.

Brandon brought his mouth down on hers.

Her pulse was already fast because she'd just barely escaped being struck by the careening sports car. But it might as well have stopped beating altogether in comparison to its speed the moment Brandon began kissing her.

Fireworks went off in her veins as his kiss registered and then deepened. Her head spun.

She'd read that exact sort of description once, had even mulled over it wistfully, despite telling herself that feelings like that didn't happen in real life. Kisses were just that. Kisses. Lips touching lips. Skin on skin. Nothing more. Kisses had no secret powers, no ability to set rockets ricocheting through the heavens and through her as they simultaneously wiped out all ability to think. That was just literary license run amok.

But here she was, having it happen. To her. One moment, she was almost roadkill, the next, soaring through the afternoon sky, no longer bound by something so mundane as a mortal body.

He made her feel positively giddy, and she absolutely loved the sensation.

The attraction Brandon had initially felt for her flared. Momentarily vulnerable by the very real possibility of losing her had his reaction been a nanosecond slower, he'd kissed her.

And discovered himself in a whole different place than he thought he would be.

Control was extremely important to Brandon, because there'd been so little of it available to him when he was younger. When he attained it, he held on to control as if it was his very reason for existing. His very lifeline.

But just for a moment now, it slipped out of his grasp as this woman took him to heights he hadn't expected and to sensations he hadn't thought possible.

It was a major revelation to him.

Coming up for air, Brandon drew back and looked in wonder at the woman he'd brought along on this little field trip. Concerned that she might have been offended, he didn't know whether or not an apology was in order. There was no way on earth he was sorry he'd kissed her. But he honestly didn't know how she might react to what had just happened.

Unable to put up with the stillness any longer, he broke it by making an apology. "Sorry," he murmured.

About? Was he sorry that he'd thrown his doors open to anyone and everyone? Or was it more personal than that? Was he sorry he kissed her?

"I already told you that you have nothing to be sorry about."

"That was before—"

He was talking about before he'd kissed her, she realized. Straightening, her eyes never leaving his, she allowed her voice to interrupt his. "But it still applies."

He relaxed a little, relieved that she wasn't annoyed, that she didn't think he had just taken advantage of her because the opportunity had presented itself. Nothing would have been further from the truth. If anything, he'd been the one to be taken advantage of. Not by her, but by his own momentary lapse into vulnerability.

He didn't like leaving himself open like that. People who were open got hurt. That was why, ordinarily, he was locked up tighter than Fort Knox. Nothing and no one got through.

Because the last time he'd allowed himself to be open, to be vulnerable, he'd lost his heart to Jean, Victoria's mother. At the time, he'd thought it was a good thing because it was for forever. Learning that "forever" was incredibly finite had been a cruel, hard lesson that had almost broken him. But he *had* learned it. It was a lesson that he meant never to forget.

But Isabelle had made him do just that, made him forget, if only for a moment.

He had to be careful that it didn't happen again. Because he knew that the consequences would be too hard for him to endure.

"About that lunch you promised me," Isabelle prodded cheerfully, sensing he needed to have his thoughts diverted. She nodded toward the old-fashioned building they'd passed at the corner.

"Right."

This time, he looked both ways before placing a hand to her back and guiding her across the street. There'd been enough risks taken for one day.

Chapter Eight

"Oh, my God, the view from here is absolutely incredible!" Isabelle cried breathlessly. "It's like looking into forever."

"Looking into forever," Brandon repeated, rolling the words around in his mind. "Might not make a bad title," he murmured, more to himself than to her.

They had had their late lunch at the restaurant, which, she'd discovered, turned out to be even more quaint on the inside than on the outside. Afterward, they'd gone across the street to take in the view. There was a charming gazebo built strictly for that purpose. It had been there, Brandon told her, for as long as anyone could remember.

The freshly repainted gray, circular structure was perched on the edge of an embankment that overlooked the beach. The ocean stretched out from there for as far as the eye could see.

It was the ocean that had captured Isabelle's attention. The waters were almost painfully blue and just slightly restless, its waves reaching out to the shore only to withdraw like a flirtatious southern belle, teasing her suitor and testing her feminine powers for the first time.

She could have stood here watching for hours. If she'd had the time.

"Do you come here often?" The moment she asked and heard her own question out loud, Isabelle had to laugh.

"What's so funny?" Brandon asked, more than a little amused. Isabelle's laugh was captivating. Captivating and innocent, like having someone take his hand and draw him into a party.

"What I just asked you, that sounded like a line a guy usually says to a girl in a bar or a club." Mocking the scenario, she made her eyebrows rise and fall wickedly before repeating the question using a far deeper voice than she had initially. "Come here often, honey?"

"As a matter of fact, I do," he purposely took on the feminine role and made his voice go up two octaves, approximating a falsetto. And then he went on more seriously in his own voice, "Driving up and down Pacific Coast Highway and looking at the ocean from here are a couple of ways I use to clear my head and get my creative juices flowing."

From out of nowhere, there was the smell of rain in the air. It rarely rained in southern California in July, so Isabelle attributed the sudden damp smell to the wind shifting, ushering in the scent of the sea.

"In your quest for creativity, do you ever walk along the beach itself?" she asked.

"That's my third way," he confirmed.

Brandon glanced down at the shoes she was wearing.

Her footwear was the one very impractical thing about her. Rather than running shoes or low, barely-there heels, Isabelle apparently favored high-heeled sandals. Granted, the heels were rather solid as opposed to stilettos, but they were still high heels. He'd never seen her wearing anything else. He'd asked her about them once, saying that he would have thought that sneakers would have worked better for her. She'd replied that she felt more stable and in control of the situation in heels. Thanks to life with his mother and Victoria, he knew better than to argue with a woman when her mind was set.

"How about it? Are you game to go for a walk on the beach now?" he asked.

Rather than answer him, Isabelle put her hand on his arm to help her maintain her balance as she slipped off her shoes. The hem of her white slacks was a hair's breadth from touching the gazebo's wooden floor.

Holding her shoes by their straps as proof, she declared, "Game!"

The quick grin that accompanied her declaration fluttered directly—and almost lethally—into Brandon's stomach.

He did his best to disregard the feeling and the very real, very strong sexual pull he experienced. This wasn't the time or the place.

"Okay, it's this way," he needlessly told her, pointing to a path that ran past another, far more image-conscious restaurant. The path was narrow and winding, and had once been painstakingly paved with colored bits of concrete, but any intended patterns that had been pressed into its surface were long gone, worn away by years of foot traffic and the sun.

The path's incline was also steep enough to make her

feel as if she could easily pitch forward if she wasn't careful or moved too quickly. She deliberately kept her gait measured and slow. To insure her stability, Isabelle slipped her arm through Brandon's.

The sand, when they finally reached it, was a pristine shade of almost white, the result of many vigilant patrons and neighbors who took pride in keeping it clean. The sand felt beguilingly warm against the soles of her bare feet the moment she took her first step. By then, Brandon had stopped to take off his own shoes—and socks—as well.

As they began to walk along the uncrowded beach, she had no doubt that the sand had found its way into the cuffs she had carefully rolled up. The thought didn't really trouble her. Being here was well worth the minor inconvenience.

With so few people around, the beach seemed somehow larger to her. As if it truly did go on forever.

Isabelle slanted a glance toward the man beside her, wondering if it made the same impression on him that it did on her.

"Does this make you feel small?" she asked, curious. "Like a speck?"

There was a hint of a smile on his lips as he shook his head. "No, it makes me feel special. Like someone seeing paradise for the first time."

She liked the way he thought. As she opened her mouth to say so, she stopped, convinced that she not only smelled rain, she felt it as well.

Was it her imagination?

Looking up at the sky, she saw no dark clouds hovering about ominously. The sky was still an exquisite shade of blue. It continued to retain its color as, out of nowhere, rain began to fall. Somewhere within the heavens, a leak had suddenly sprung.

Grabbing her hand, Brandon made a mad dash back up to the winding path.

It required more energy to go up than come down, especially at a pace that was three times as fast. As if determined to keep pace, the rain seemed to increase with every step they took until they finally made it up to the shelter of the gazebo.

"I think I just burned off dessert," Isabelle commented, doing her best to regulate her breathing once more.

As they stood beneath the gazebo's wooden roof, the sun shower turned noisy. Instead of raindrops, Isabelle thought she heard the roof being pelted. *Really* pelted. She looked at Brandon quizzically.

"Is that hail?" she asked him.

"Sounds like it," he answered. "Looks like it, too," he added, pointing to the ground behind them just outside the gazebo. A blanket of icy drops was swiftly forming, covering the grass between the gazebo and the sidewalk.

Isabelle brushed her wet bangs away from her eyes. She had to look a mess, she suddenly realized. Dropping her shoes to the floor, she stepped into them, then ran her hands up and down her arms, brushing away some of the raindrops.

"God, I think I'm soaked to the bone," she observed.

Rather than stare at her very wet body and the way her cotton blouse clung to her upper torso as if she was a contestant in a wet T-shirt contest, Brandon made himself look at her face.

He dug into his back pocket and took out his neatly

folded handkerchief and, to the obvious surprise registered in her eyes, carefully wiped the moisture from her face.

Brandon held out the handkerchief to her, and she graciously took it.

She dabbed at her throat and the damp swell just above her breasts. At that point, the handkerchief was too wet to do any more good.

She flashed a smile at Brandon as she offered the handkerchief back to him. "Thanks. I feel totally dry now."

He laughed, slipping the wet handkerchief into his wetter jeans. Even as he did so, they could see that the hailstorm had all but abated.

In the next few minutes, the sun shower retreated, as well.

Less than fifteen minutes after the rain had started, it dispersed. Except for the few remaining patches of hail clumped together here and there on the ground, it was as if they'd both just shared a mutual hallucination.

"What *was* that?" she asked Brandon, peering up uncertainly at the blue sky.

He could recall experiencing maybe three hail storms in his lifetime, none of them while the sky was a crystal clear blue.

"I'm not too sure," he admitted. "But as long as a torrent of frogs doesn't start falling from the sky, I'd venture to say that things are still pretty good and that God's not mad at us."

"Nice to know," she murmured.

It was only now, in retrospect, that she realized that Brandon had grabbed her hand to make sure she kept up as he'd run back for shelter. Taking her hand rather than silently declaring, solely by his actions, that it was every man—and woman—for him-or-herself.

The man was chivalrous under fire, as well as heart-throb handsome.

Perfect in every way, Isabelle couldn't help thinking. So far, she hadn't found any flaws in the man. He was good to his mother, clearly loved his child, had a sense of humor and was witty and intelligent. The perfect package.

But, she knew, remembering her father and the aura that he had shattered, no man was perfect.

What was Brandon Slade's flaw? she couldn't help wondering.

So far, she hadn't seen evidence of any shortcoming, and that just wasn't possible. Men as seemingly perfect as Brandon Slade existed in fairy tales and all answered to the same name: Prince Charming. In other words, they were fictional characters who weren't even awarded a moniker because why waste a perfectly good name on a character who hadn't a prayer of existing in the real world?

Brandon's deep voice broke into her thoughts. "Maybe we'd better make our getaway while the getting's good," he suggested. "In case the rain comes back. Unless you want to stay here for a while longer," he tacked on. He watched her, waiting.

Much as she would have liked to remain here with him, she knew she had to be getting back. By the time they would reach his house, it would be time for his mother's next exercise session. As tempting as the thought of spending more time with him right here was, she had to keep in mind why she was remotely a tempo-rary part of Brandon Slade's world in the first place.

It was *not* to dash along the beach, trying to outrun the rain.

But she had to be honest. "I'd love to," she told him. "But your mother should have another PT session at three. All things considered—" which was a very polite way of glossing over the actress's bombastic personality and her way of taking charge of any given situation no matter what "—your mother's doing rather well. I'd hate to interrupt her progress because I like feeling sand between my toes." She flashed a grin at him. "Or running from a sun shower."

Brandon inclined his head. He couldn't help wondering, though, if Isabelle had a clue how infectious her grin was. "Home it is."

Home.

For a tiny moment, the word embraced her, as if it was not just his home but hers, too. The idea warmed her and brought a smile to her inner core.

You've got a perfectly nice home of your own, remember? The small voice in her head—her common sense she liked to think—sounded almost exasperated with her.

She had to be careful, Isabelle warned herself. She had a tendency to get carried away. A tendency to let her imagination get the better of her. Brandon had made her feel welcome and was continuing to do so, but that was just his way. *She* was the hired help. A trained, highly professional physical therapist, but still the hired help.

She had to remember that. Letting herself believe anything else was just asking for trouble. Although that had never happened before with work, she had an uneasy feeling things were different now.

Because the circumstances were different and Brandon had entered her world.

He hasn't entered your world, idiot. You've entered his. The second his mother's more flexible, you're history, just someone that he knows.

There were times when she just hated being right.

"You've gotten very quiet," Brandon observed as they got into the car. He'd handed her the oversize beach towel he'd found in his trunk and she'd wrapped it around herself. "Is something wrong?" he asked.

"No, I'm just thinking about your mother's exercise program," she lied. It was a handy excuse to fall back on, also pretty transparent, she thought, but she really wasn't versed in lying. She'd never had a reason to lie before.

Putting the key into the ignition, Brandon paused for a moment, scrutinizing her.

And looking right through her, Isabelle thought.

"Lucky for you, Pinocchio is just a fairy tale," he told her, turning the key. The SUV's engine rumbled to life.

She squared her shoulders defensively, even as she knew there was no point. He was apparently on to her. "Are you saying you think I'm lying?"

"Just making an observation," Brandon answered innocently. And then, more seriously, he said, "And being a little worried."

"Worried?" she repeated. What was he worried about? His mother? He had no reason to be worried in that department. "Don't be," she told him, then went on to add, "I already told you, your mother's doing fine—"

He cut her short before she could begin to elaborate. "Yes, I know."

Okay, she was confused, not to mention lost. "Then why…?"

Pulling out of the parking space, he waited until he had straightened the wheel and driven to the corner before continuing. "I was referring to you."

"Me?" Now she was really confused. "You're worried about me? Why?"

This was unfamiliar ground for him. But then, he didn't usually venture into this kind of territory. "I was worried that maybe, because of what happened earlier, you'd want to quit."

"What happened earlier?" she repeated, thinking he was referring to getting soaked in the shower. "No offense intended, Brandon. You're a very famous man and all, but I don't think you have what it takes to be responsible for a sudden drastic shift in the weather."

"Earlier than that," was all he said as he began to drive back up Pacific Coast Highway. Quaint little shops whizzed by in reverse as he made his way back to Mac-Arthur Boulevard and Newport Beach.

That only left one thing. Her eyes widened in amazement. "You think I'd quit because you kissed me? Or because you stopped?" she added, a whimsical smile playing on her lips.

When she mentioned the latter, he knew he was on safer ground. A note of relief slipped into his countenance. Granted, he could always find another physical therapist for his mother—it wasn't as if Isabelle was the only one available on the North American continent—but his mother liked the woman, and that in itself was a rarity. Besides, he liked her, as well, and it wasn't exactly a hardship having her around for a while longer.

"Then we're okay?" he asked for form's sake.

"We're fine," she answered. "Trust me, if you'd done something I didn't like, I wouldn't have meekly let it happen—or held my tongue. I might look like one, but I'm not a shy wallflower."

He thought of the way she'd driven like a speed demon to get back to his house so he could start getting feeling back in his legs. "No," he agreed, "you're not. And for the record—"

He stopped abruptly as he began to maneuver his vehicle around a moving truck that hogged the entire road.

Impatient, Isabelle forced herself to wait until he cleared the truck, then pressed, "Yes?"

"For the record," he repeated, "you don't look like any wallflower I ever encountered." Slanting a glance in her direction, he glimpsed her grin. "Why would you even say that?" he asked. "Who told you that you look like a wallflower?"

"Zoe. My sister," she added in case he'd forgotten her sister's name.

"I know who Zoe is," he told her. He had a great memory when it came to names, people and places. "What you didn't mention, however, was that she was blind."

Her smile blossomed into a full, wide, pleased grin. "She just worries about me," she said by way of excusing her sister. "She wants me to make 'the best' of my 'assets' so that I don't wind up growing old alone."

"I think you're alone because you want to be," Brandon told her, making a judgment call. "*Not* because you have to be."

That was all very sweet, but he was missing a very salient point. She knew it wasn't exactly prudent to make the admission, but she'd never been one to play games. "I'm not exactly beating off men with a stick here."

Having temporarily put himself in her place, something he did whenever he was trying to understand someone's motivation, Brandon had an explanation.

"That's because you've been burying yourself in your work." He spared her another glance. "By choice, I'm guessing."

Was that a lucky guess, or was he just being polite? Either way, the man had managed to hit awfully close to the actual truth. She thought of denying it, but she had a feeling it would do no good. He was right, and she sensed that he knew it. But, she was willing to bet, he didn't know why she wasn't in the market for a relationship—and she intended to keep that to herself.

"When did I tell you that I wanted my fortune told?" she asked wryly.

"Consider it a bonus for working with my mother. Or," he went on, giving her another way to view this, "you could consider this as the result of being around a writer who likes to stay on his toes by dissecting situations and people."

No, she thought, "bonus" was the way she viewed the outing they'd just had—and most of all, it was the word she applied to the kiss they'd shared. Both, in their own way, were precious to her.

And, more than likely, a one-time-only kind thing. She didn't foresee circumstances arranging themselves so that she found herself on the receiving end of affection any time in the near future.

Or ever.

"I'll keep that in mind," she murmured.

It occurred to Brandon that he had never heard that particular sentence sound so very pregnant with possibilities before.

Or promise.

But then, he reminded himself, he'd only known Isabelle for a very short amount of time.

Chapter Nine

After that initial foray into Brandon's creative process, much to her surprise and delight, Isabelle found herself being drawn further and further into the man's literary world.

To her the whole process was exciting beyond words. But, at the same time, she didn't want him to think of her as some sort of a wide-eyed groupie. To that end, she'd already made up her mind to turn down his next invitation.

Except that the next one was to attend a reception scheduled to be held directly after his book signing at one of the local branches of a large national bookstore chain. When he asked her if she wanted to attend, the word "no" hovered on her lips. However, it never actually emerged. She'd swallowed it the moment Brandon began to describe the event to her. Within moments she knew that she couldn't pass up something like this.

There would never be another opportunity to attend a reception like this as a guest of the author.

Besides, she discovered that refusing him was next to impossible for her.

Especially since he began by saying he'd take her attendance as a personal favor because she would be keeping an eye on his daughter *and* his mother, both of whom were coming to the signing and the reception.

She couldn't say no after that.

And that was why the following afternoon, during a break between Anastasia's morning and afternoon therapy sessions, found her in the nearby shopping mall. Since the reception was taking place after five, she was in the market for a simple black dress that promised to be anything *but* simple.

There was nothing simple about the price tag attached to the dress. But, since this was a once-in-a-lifetime situation, Isabelle closed her eyes and thrust her credit card toward the sales clerk. The slinky little number, which fit her as if it had been created with her in mind, easily cost almost as much as the rest of the clothes hanging in her closet put together.

But as Isabelle surveyed herself in the mirror the evening of the big event, she felt it was worth the price.

It was difficult for her not to allow her imagination to take flight, creating fanciful scenarios that had built on that afternoon they had spent at Laguna Beach.

She had to keep reminding herself that she was going to the signing and the reception afterward not as Brandon's friend, not even as a fan of his work, but in the capacity of his mother's physical therapist. She was going for a very legitimate reason: to help Victoria keep an eye on her grandmother because Anastasia Del Vecchio had a tendency to overdo things and none of them wanted the actress to jeopardize the progress she'd made so far.

It was a given that the world-famous cinema icon did nothing by half measures. Since she hadn't fully bounced back from her surgery yet, getting overly tired was definitely not advisable. Which meant that she, Isabelle Sinclair, would have to watch the woman like a hawk. She knew that definitely would not endear her to the actress. Anastasia balked at restrictions, even those implemented for her own good. It was obvious that she still thought of herself as a woman in her early thirties, able to do whatever it was she set her mind to do.

But nothing, Isabelle thought, turning around slowly to view herself from as many different angles as humanly possible, said she couldn't look good while acting as Anastasia's keeper.

The reflection looking back at her was *damn* good.

Rather than the utilitarian style she wore most days, with her hair pulled back away from her face, Isabelle kept her hair down. And, except for one small ornamental comb strategically positioned over her right ear, her hair was free to swing about.

"This is as good as it gets," she declared under her breath. No amount of extra fussing would improve on what she saw.

Not that there was a need for improvement.

Stepping into black sling-back sandals that added four inches to her height, Isabelle picked up her small black purse and slipped the thin strap over her shoulder. She would have preferred a clutch purse, but there was no way one of those would accommodate the absolute minimum of things she considered vital for functioning.

The next size up barely did that, but, with some strategic packing and squeezing in the right places, the purse accommodated what she needed and still allowed her to snap the clasp shut.

Isabelle paused for a second just shy of the doorway, took a deep breath to center herself and then let it go.

Okay, here I come, ready or not, she silently declared.

Stepping out into the hallway, she heard Brandon, already downstairs from the sound of it, calling for everyone to come together.

Clapping his hands, he called up the stairs. "Let's go, let's go, ladies. I don't want to be late for my own signing."

"Why not?" Anastasia asked. She took the stairs down seemingly without effort, which pleased Isabelle no end. Going up and down the stairs was actually a good form of exercise for the woman—as long as she was careful not to move too fast. "This way, you can make an entrance. An entrance with a beautiful woman on each arm," she added with a flourish as she came to stand at the bottom of the stairs.

"Dramatic entrances are for you, Mother," Brandon answered with patient affection. "I'm just happy nobody's throwing any rotten fruit or vegetables at me."

"They never did that," Victoria spoke up loyally, then paused, curious since her father *had* brought it up. "Did they?"

"No." He laughed, about to ruffle her hair, then remembered that it had been painstakingly arranged by Olga, his mother's hairstylist these past ten years and the only one she would even *allow* to touch her hair. Ever tactful, Brandon dropped his hand to his side. "Okay, I count two. Where's Isabelle?" he asked, glancing at his watch again.

"Right here," Isabelle answered, addressing him from

the top of the stairs. It was no easy feat considering that her heart was in her throat, as well.

"Good," he declared, "because we have to get… going."

The last word came out in slow motion because he'd just looked up, following the sound of her voice, and had completely lost the thread of his thoughts. And lost his breath as well, at least temporarily, as his eyes traveled up and down the length of her. The slinky black garment stopped several good inches short of her knees, caressing her thighs with each step she took down. Making him long to do the same.

She smiled, pleased at the expression on his face. "You're staring," she pointed out.

"That's because I've never seen your legs before. I mean, without pants on." That didn't sound right. "Your pants." That sounded even worse. "I mean—"

Anastasia shook her head. "Listen to the world-famous writer, tripping over his own tongue."

Isabelle saw the mesmerized look in Brandon's eyes, and it triggered an excitement within her she hadn't been prepared for. "I don't mind," she said, her voice low as her eyes met his.

"Were your legs always that long?" he asked, still very much captivated by the image she projected.

"Always," she assured him.

Brandon took in a long breath, then let it out again. Slowly. His pulse beat erratically, but mercifully, began to settle down. "Funny, I would have thought I would have noticed that," he commented.

Anastasia was the one to finally break the spell. She let out a deep stage sigh. "Of course her legs are the same length as always. Really, Brandon," the older woman chided, shaking her head. "Now, if you're finished fantasizing, you have a signing to get to. The one you didn't want to be late for, remember?" his mother reminded him with just a touch of sarcasm.

The venerable actress gave no indication that she was pleased at his reaction to the young woman she had already given her seal of approval to. Anastasia knew her son well enough to realize that if she appeared to be pushing Isabelle toward him or him toward her, Brandon would find a reason to suddenly take off, leaving the house and the vicinity for long, long stretches of time.

He refused to be manipulated, and in that, he was very much his mother's son, she thought with pride. Fortunately, she was better at manipulation than he suspected.

So, for now, it would appear to be business as usual for her. That meant focusing on herself and the world as it revolved around her.

Not too much of a stretch, Anastasia silently granted. But Lord, she really did feel impatient. More than anything else, she wanted the blinders to be lifted from her son's eyes so he could *see* for himself how very perfect this young woman was for him.

After all, he wasn't getting any younger, and she wanted to make certain that both he and Victoria had someone in their lives who was looking after them while she was away.

She couldn't be expected to put her own life on hold indefinitely, Anastasia thought. The public would grow weary of waiting and find someone else to adore. And she absolutely *refused* to be replaced so easily.

So she pretended to glance at Isabelle and gave her only a short, distracted nod of approval. "You look very nice, dear. As do we all." She smiled at Victoria to make her point.

Her granddaughter looked so grown up, Anastasia thought. Where had that adorable, pigtailed little girl gone? And who was this mature-looking young lady who'd come in her place? Time went by too quickly.

"Now, can we get going before the people waiting on you decide that they like someone else, someone more punctual," Anastasia emphasized, "someone better?"

"Yes, Mother," Brandon murmured, amused since, for the most part, he and Victoria spent a great deal of time waiting on her.

With a gallant little bow, Brandon offered her the crook of his arm for support.

Anastasia sniffed and waved him away.

"I am perfectly capable of walking out the door on my own," she informed him haughtily. "Besides, if I do need someone's assistance, I have Victoria." She smiled at her granddaughter. "If you really want to play the role of a gentleman and a scholar, offer your arm to Isabelle there." The actress waved him toward the other woman. "She's the one wearing impossibly high heels." Even as she made the observation, the older woman critically narrowed her eyes as she looked down at the strappy footwear her physical therapist sported.

"You heard her," Brandon said to Isabelle, moving to the side in order to offer his arm to her.

"If you're waiting for a pratfall, I'm afraid you have a long wait," Isabelle informed him as she slipped her own arm through the crook of his. "I've gotten pretty good at moving rather quickly in high heels."

He was grinning at her before he realized it. "I'll challenge you to a foot race after the reception," he offered.

Amusement rose in her eyes. "All right, Brandon, I'll just take that challenge."

Anastasia hung back by several steps, observing what she considered to be her handiwork, even if it began by accident because she had complained to the right person. She had to remember to send more business Cecilia's way, Anastasia told herself, making a mental note.

"They make a nice couple," Victoria whispered to her.

The actress glanced at her granddaughter. There were times she forgot that the girl was actually as young as she was. But that was only chronologically. Anastasia was certain that, at birth, Victoria had been granted an old soul.

It was, she supposed, a consolation prize of sorts, to make up for the fact that the woman who had given birth to Victoria chose to turn her back on the small miracle she'd brought into the world.

The little witch has no idea what she's missing out on, Anastasia thought, not for the first time. And she, for one, was glad that Jean was gone. Both Brandon and Victoria deserved better.

She smiled at her granddaughter. "Yes," Anastasia whispered back. "They do."

Isabelle had no idea that a bookstore this size—and it was by no means tiny—could actually pack in this many people. It seemed as if every possibly available space in the store had been taken up by adoring Brandon Slade fans.

For the most part, Isabelle observed, the crowd was comprised of women. And not just women of a certain age, but of all ages. Young ones, old ones, tall ones, short ones, fashionably dressed or looking as if they'd just jumped out of bed or had come running over from their local gyms, sweaty and eager—they were all here.

Here and clutching Brandon's newest hardcover to their chests as they stood in what appeared to be an extremely long, winding and seemingly endless line. They were all patiently—or not so patiently—waiting for their ten seconds of one-on-one time with Brandon Slade. At this point they would get a personalized autograph jotted down within the front pages of this newest tome, which they would treasure and sigh over in the days to come.

Several times Isabelle found that if she hadn't staunchly held her ground where she was—near Brandon—she would have been either elbowed or pushed outright to the side by some overeager fan. Apparently they all wanted to get close to, if not their favorite author, at least the best-looking one they'd seen up close and personal.

Anastasia gestured for her to stand beside her and Victoria, directly behind Brandon's table. Bypassing another handful of fans, Isabelle managed to get over to where the actress and her granddaughter were standing.

"The madness is all taking place in front of Brandon, not back here," Anastasia assured her confidently. "This isn't my first signing," she added.

Isabelle noticed the way Brandon's agent, Maura Reynolds, hovered close to his side, a position she'd been in for the past ninety minutes. The other woman had assumed that place immediately following the reading he'd given from the first chapter of his new book. Isabelle couldn't help wondering if Maura, who was clearly older than her prize client, had a crush on Brandon the way so many of his fans appeared to.

Needing a diversion, Isabelle turned toward Brandon's mother. "Is it always this crazy?" she asked.

Anastasia waved a well-manicured hand indulgently

about the crowd. "It's been worse, trust me," the actress told her, adding after a beat, "it's also been *much* worse." When Isabelle raised her eyebrows quizzically, the woman elaborated. "Those were the signings when no one came. It took his first book a while to catch on." Anastasia leaned in so that she didn't have to raise her voice—or have Brandon overhear her. "Personally, I think his looks had a lot to do with those initial sales," she confided.

"*And* he got better," Victoria interjected loyally, referring to her father's second book. It was all speculation on her part since she had been far too young at the time to know any of the actual details.

"Yes, he did," Anastasia agreed—whether because she meant it or was humoring her beloved granddaughter was hard to say, Isabelle thought. But the enthusiasm in the older woman's voice would have been the same either way and that was all that counted. It was apparent that in her own, very dramatic way, Anastasia Del Vecchio loved her son very much, even though she found ways to bedevil the ego she feared he'd develop.

Isabelle smiled at the exchange between grandmother and granddaughter.

The next moment, her smile faded as a woman in the line before Brandon's table caught her attention.

A rather statuesque woman, whose long, straight hair was just possibly the palest shade of blond she had ever seen, leaned forward over Brandon's table.

"I'd like an autograph, please," she murmured in a deliberately melodic voice that sounded as if it had been dipped in honey.

"That's what I'm here for," Brandon answered, his pen poised. "Who shall I make it out to?" As he asked the question, he reached for the book she was holding that he assumed she'd just purchased.

But the woman shook her head. Placing the book on the table, she put her hands on top of it and leaned even farther forward. Her blue silk blouse, already unbuttoned farther than Isabelle felt was decently acceptable, strained against the weight of two very ripe breasts that were ready to make a break for it at any moment.

"No, not the book," she said in what could only be termed a Marilyn Monroe whisper. "I want you to sign *here*," she instructed with a wicked, come-hither smile. "Make it out to 'Annaliese, with love and appreciation, Brandon Slade.'" She ended her instructions with a frothy giggle.

As Isabelle watched, waiting to see what he was going to do, Brandon remained completely unflappable. He returned "Annaliese's" smile, but he shook his head.

"I'm sorry, but I can't. I'm afraid that my pen only writes on paper," he apologized.

Apparently prepared and very much undaunted, the would-be Marilyn Monroe produced a laundry marker from her purse.

"How about this?" she suggested. "It's supposed to write on *anything*," she breathed.

For a moment, it looked to Isabelle as if Brandon would give in and sign his autograph on the young woman's very ample chest. But then, to her relief and surprise, he said, "How about I put it someplace where it isn't going to be washed off when you take your next shower?"

By his satisfied expression he knew he had the young woman. She would either say she didn't intend to ever shower again, which was off-putting by anyone's standards, or she'd have to indicate that she didn't care if the autograph lasted or not, which was ultimately an insult to the man she was trying to flatter.

With a sigh, the woman called Annaliese straightened and allowed the fabric of her blouse to fall back into place, covering at least part of her cleavage. With a pout, she held up the book she'd had to purchase in order to take her place in line to begin with.

"Okay."

Brandon took extra time and made sure that the message he wrote down was more than just the standard "To my friend So-and-So—"

The young woman's disappointment faded away as she retreated from the line, reading his message and smiling to herself.

"Nicely done," Isabelle murmured. She'd made the observation under her breath, and it was intended strictly for herself.

Despite that, Brandon had apparently heard her above the din and looked at her over his shoulder.

He flashed a grin at her and said, "Thanks," before turning back to autograph his book for the next person in line.

So why did that simple one word acknowledgement make her feel as if someone had just lit a fire inside of her? A fire that was warming up every single part of her at once.

She had no answer for that.

Yet.

Chapter Ten

The reception gave no indication that it was about to wind down any time soon. Instead, it appeared to have comfortably settled into a rhythm and gave every indication of going on for hours, conversation and wine flowing effortlessly.

Hired to cater the event, Theresa Manetti made sure that the serving platters on the buffet table were never empty and that all the glasses that were in play were continually being refilled. She had a reputation to maintain.

But aside from that, being here also allowed her the opportunity to covertly observe the young woman she had "unofficially" made her newest project. Isabelle Sinclair had certainly come a long way from the woman she'd glimpsed just a short while ago. The other one had been pretty in a shy, retiring way. This woman was vivacious. A "knockout" as her father used to say, Theresa thought with a fond smile.

Seeing Isabelle interacting with Brandon Slade gave Theresa every hope that this particular pairing she had undertaken would turn out to be as successful as the handful of others she, Maizie and Cecilia had gotten involved with. So far, their record was five out of five. This, she thought with a smile, just might be lucky number six.

Approximately ninety minutes into the reception, Anastasia, with Victoria in tow, made her way over to her son. As always, he was surrounded by a number of women of various ages. This time, he was telling his adoring fans the story of how he'd received the news of his first book making it to the *New York Times* bestseller list.

"At first I thought it was one of my friends, making a crank call and pulling my leg. So I hung up. After the person called back a second time, I placed my own call to my agent and got the same person who very coldly informed me that my agent was in a meeting and she couldn't be disturbed, but she'd asked him—turns out he was her assistant—to call me with the good news. He sounded very put out. I spent the next fifteen minutes apologizing to him—and then the next forty-eight hours celebrating," he concluded with a grin.

It was clear that his audience was eager for another anecdote. But the moment he saw his mother approaching with Victoria, Brandon politely extricated himself from the tight circle of women, promising to return with another story "later."

Crossing to his mother, who was clearly going somewhere, he asked, "What's up?" He looked from his mother to his daughter, waiting for an answer.

"Brandon, it's getting late. It might not be a school night, but Victoria and I are going home," his mother announced.

He could remember when his mother could party not just all night long but several days running, as well. Back in those days, she'd been unharnessed energy and had given no indication of ever slowing down or growing tired.

Age was a bear, he thought with a touch of sadness. For form's sake, because he knew she'd refuse to admit she was tired, he asked his mother, "Is anything wrong?"

"No, nothing's wrong. But it's past Victoria's bedtime and I don't want her overdoing it," Anastasia elaborated.

The excuse was paper-thin, but he saw no reason to let her know that he saw through it. In order to spare his mother's pride, Brandon played along. He glanced over his shoulder at the circle of women he'd just left. They were still waiting for him. One of the women waved at him.

Danger, Will Robinson, Danger, he thought, whimsically calling to mind a famous catch phrase from a bygone era. "Maybe I should go, too," he said to his mother.

Anastasia looked genuinely horrified. "No, no, you and Isabelle stay here," she insisted, patting his hand. "Enjoy yourselves."

"Isabelle's not going with you?" Sexy or not, the woman *was* his mother's physical therapist and as such should really be accompanying her, not him, Brandon thought.

"Why should she?" Anastasia asked, surprised that he would even suggest such a thing. "It only takes one of us to make sure Victoria goes to bed," she said, draping an arm around the girl's slender shoulders.

Brandon noticed that his daughter looked as if she wanted to protest but was prudent enough not to. Wise beyond her years, that girl, he thought with pride.

Digging into his pocket, he located his keys. Brandon took them out and held them out to his mother. He knew that her surgeon had just cleared her to drive yesterday. He assumed she was eager to get back behind the wheel again. Control was all important to his mother, it always had been. "Take my car, then."

She pushed his hand—and the keys—back. "No need. Maura is taking us home," she told him, referring to his agent. "She was planning on leaving early anyway." Anastasia waved her hand vaguely. "Something about having to take an early phone call tomorrow. I don't know," she confessed. "I wasn't really listening. You know how she can go on and on."

His agent would just drop his mother off at the curb, never leaving her vehicle. He wasn't sure if he was happy with that. "You'll be all right, going home by yourself?" he questioned.

"I won't be by myself," Anastasia reminded him, then looked toward her granddaughter. "I have Victoria. What more could I ask for?"

Brandon smiled. There were indeed times when it felt as if Victoria was the adult and his mother, and occasionally, he supposed, he as well, were the children. His daughter was born with an old soul, which was fortunate for him because he wouldn't have known what to do with a typical rebellious teenager.

Walking in at the tail end of the conversation, Isabelle

joined Brandon and his family. "I should be going with you," she told the actress.

That was exactly what Anastasia *didn't* want. She wanted the two of them to be alone together—as alone as was possible in the middle of a packed reception.

"Nonsense, dear. This is the shank of the evening for you and you're only young once—trust me on this." The woman patted Isabelle's cheek with her heavily ringed hand. "Enjoy yourself. Keep an eye out for Brandon and make sure some overendowed, eager fan doesn't get it into her head to make off with him," she requested. "He has trouble saying 'no.' To anyone except his poor mother."

Brandon laughed. "There's absolutely nothing 'poor' about you, Mother."

Anastasia took it as her due. "Thank you, dear." As she spoke, she looked around for Brandon's agent. "Ah, there she is. Maura," she called out, raising her arm and waving from side to side to catch the woman's attention. "We're ready to go."

His agent, a short, sensible-looking woman wearing a blue sequined dress that transformed her squat torso into a walking blue flame, nodded.

"Then let's go." She put a hand to the small of each of their backs. "I'm parked in the first row," she informed her charges as she herded them both off.

Now what? Isabelle wondered.

She looked after the departing actress, clearly torn between her sense of duty and a very strong streak of desire, a streak that insisted on growing with every breath she took.

"I really should go with her," she murmured to Brandon.

"No, you shouldn't," he contradicted. She looked

at him, puzzled. "It took me a while to get versed in Anastasia-speak but if she tells you she wants you to stay, then she wants you to stay. Really."

Isabelle still had her doubts as she watched the two women and Victoria weave their way through the crowd and inch over to the front of the bookstore. "She's leaving because she's tired—"

"Which is exactly why you shouldn't accompany her," he pointed out. "She's using Victoria as an excuse to leave. This way, she can slip into bed without damaging her reputation as the queen of the all nighters. If you go with her, she'll be forced to stay up and pretend that she could have gone on all night—when she couldn't."

"That's pretty convoluted." But, she supposed, in an odd sort of way, that did make sense.

"So's my mother," he pointed out. "Trust me, it's better this way. Besides, she's just a little tired, it's not like she's going to need a blood transfusion once she's home. There's no real reason for you to go with her." It occurred to Brandon, as he made the case for her to stay, that there could be another reason why Isabelle might be trying to leave. "Unless you don't want to stay."

"Not want to stay?" she echoed. How could he even *think* such a thing? Maybe this was old hat to Brandon but not to her. "I'm feeling a little like Cinderella at the ball. I don't get to go to many parties in my line of work," she told him, silently adding that, counting this one, it brought the grand total up to one—if she didn't count the one that Zoe'd thrown to celebrate their fifth year in business last month.

"Then I'm not making you remain against your will," he concluded. "Good. Feeling adventurous?" he asked completely out of the blue. There was amusement in his sky blue eyes.

Isabelle could feel her heart suddenly hitching in her throat even though there was no logical reason why it should.

"Okay," she replied tentatively, stretching the word out.

He grinned. "Can I interest you in sampling some appetizers with me?" He indicated the center of the buffet table against the far wall.

He, Isabelle thought, could interest her in sampling chocolate-covered worms. The idea didn't even make her cringe. Since she'd taken on the famous screen icon's case, it had all seemed like one giant adventure to her, and she secretly hoped it would never end, even though she knew it had to.

There were less than three weeks left before the tour for Anastasia's play, *A Little Night Music,* was to begin. That was the deadline she'd been given to get the actress into "top dancing condition."

Which meant that there were less than three weeks for her to be part of this world that seemed like a fairy tale come true to her.

She realized that she hadn't answered Brandon and he was still waiting. "Sure, why not?" she said gamely.

The three large platters of artfully arranged appetizers formed an exotic array. They each took five different ones, giving them a total of ten to sample.

"Oh, wow, you have to try this one," Brandon enthused, after taking a small bite of an appetizer that, in Isabelle's estimation, apparently tasted far better than it looked.

Rather than have her go back to the table to get one of her own, Brandon held out the second half of the one he'd sampled and fed it to her.

She hardly tasted it.

All of her senses were otherwise occupied as the intimate moment—despite the people milling all around them—registered all the way into the deep recesses of her soul.

For just that one precious moment, there was nothing and no one else but the two of them and a canapé that involved marinated chicken, guacamole and some unknown, sweet ingredient that seemed to explode on her tongue into a wild spectrum of flavors.

Not the smallest of which was desire.

Breathe! Breathe, damn it, or you're going to pass out right here at his feet, dummy, she chided herself as she realized that she'd literally stopped exhaling for more than just a beat.

"Good?" he asked, peering closely at her face.

Exquisite. Beyond anything I've ever felt. Isabelle nodded her response, not trusting her voice to come out in anything except an unintelligible squeak.

He took another two canapés and slipped them onto his plate, intent on sharing each with her. "I don't know who the caterer is, but I'm having them do my Christmas party this year," he declared. "By the way, you're invited."

It was an offhanded invitation that she was certain he forgot the moment he offered it. Surely he'd forget by the time the season rolled around.

But she never would.

They wound up staying until the very end. Brandon, the epitome of energy, gave every indication of going on forever. And when the reception finally did wind down and then break up, Brandon looked almost sorry that the party was over.

As he said his goodbyes to the bookstore owner, a

heavyset man who pumped his hand and thanked him twice over for coming, Brandon turned toward Isabelle. All sorts of ideas were forming in his head.

She was even more beautiful right now than she'd been at the beginning of the evening—and it wasn't the wine talking because he hadn't had any for the past hour and a half. He hadn't had much before then, either. He liked having a clear head.

Isabelle was fumbling with her shawl, and he slipped it around her shoulders for her, his fingers brushing against her arm's bare skin.

The contact was electrifying. He wondered if she'd felt it, too.

"I don't feel like going home just yet," he told her. "You up for a walk on the beach?"

She resisted the urge to tell him that if he wanted to run off to the circus, she was up for that, too. Instead, she said, "That sounds very nice. Count me in," and left it at that.

The sound of the ocean, its waves sliding in to flirt with the shore before coquettishly withdrawing, promised to have a very soothing effect. She welcomed the thought. Right now she felt as if she was still fully charged and about to go off like a misfired rocket at any moment.

The beach, as it turned out, was located not that far from the bookstore. They gained access to it by taking a path that started directly behind the store and cut across an alley between two summer homes before it finally brought them straight down to the beach.

There was a full moon out, casting its light onto the waters.

Just for us, she thought, watching the moonbeams glimmer along the dark waters.

"There's a full moon out tonight," she commented.

"Like it?" Brandon asked, weaving his fingers through her hand as he deadpanned, "I ordered ahead for it."

She looked at him for a long moment. The man was heart-stoppingly gorgeous, she thought, not for the first time. "I guess you can get pretty much anything you want," she speculated, only half tongue in cheek.

"Tell you the truth, I *have* pretty much everything I want." And then, as if to prove it, he enumerated. "I've got the career I've always wanted. A really terrific daughter I sometimes feel I don't deserve and then, of course, there's Mother."

A fond smile curved his generous mouth as a slightly distant look came into his eyes. "She's a hoot and I can't say she's even remotely typical, but life with her was an education from the very first moment. I don't think I'd be where I am if I'd had a typical mother."

He was forgetting about his determination, about his drive. "I think you might be," she told him.

"Oh?" he asked, curious. "And why's that?"

It was hard for her to think, to complete a thought, when he held her hand like that.

"Because we all carry the seeds inside of us of what we are and what we have the potential to become." She warmed to her subject. "You take two people with the same set of circumstances in their background. One grows up to be a success, the other becomes a bitter, complaining failure, blaming everyone else for the fact that he never got anywhere in life instead of putting the blame where it belongs. At his own feet. The only difference between them is one is motivated to make something of himself, maybe even *despite* his famous parents, the other feels he had three strikes against him from the very start and doesn't even try."

Brandon wondered if that comparison was made for his benefit. "Let me guess, you minored in psychology."

Only if she expanded her campus to include her life. "No, but your mother isn't the first celebrity I've worked with." There were so many children of privilege who had the air of entitlement about them. He had no idea how lucky he was to have Victoria turn out the way she had—or maybe Victoria was the lucky one to have a parent like Brandon raising her. He might be her father, but part of him was also her best friend—a position she knew he was going to miss in the years ahead after the girl had grown up. "You get to see a lot in my line of work," she said vaguely.

The writer in him prompted Brandon to ask, "Anything you can talk about?"

He sounded so interested, she couldn't just turn him down flat.

"A couple," she allowed. "Without naming names."

He shook his head. "Not interested in names, just situations," he told her. "I write fiction, not a gossip column—although, at times, that seems to be one and the same," he commented.

"As long as I don't have to use real names, then sure."

And as they walked, she talked, telling him about a couple of her more challenging cases and the family dynamics that went along with them that she'd found intriguing. When she worked with a client, Isabelle liked to think she worked with the whole person, not just his or her condition. That involved getting to know and working with the client's family—such as it was. At times, she thought the client would be better off without his or her family.

That wasn't the case here, she mused. All three family members were who they were because of the effect they had on one another.

Brandon proved to be a very attentive audience, quietly listening to her as she talked and only speaking to ask an occasional question whenever she paused.

When she came to the end of the third case she shared with him, Isabelle stopped to "scrutinize" her audience. She was convinced that Brandon was just being polite, letting her ramble on.

"You can't possibly find all this interesting," she protested.

"Yes, I can," he countered.

And the stories weren't the only thing he found interesting, Brandon added silently. As he listened to her talk about her interactions with the families of some of her clients, Brandon found himself also thinking about the woman, as well.

Thinking about her and discovering that he hadn't just imagined it. He was very much attracted to her. Strongly.

At that point, they'd already turned around and were on their way back to the bookstore. He'd left his gleaming white vehicle parked in the lot behind the chain store.

Approximately half a block away from the bookstore, he abruptly stopped walking. She watched him carefully, but said nothing.

"Would you mind if I kissed you?" he asked.

Mind? It was all she'd been thinking about for the past ten minutes. So much so that it had become difficult for her to hold on to her train of thought and continue with her story.

"You didn't ask the first time," she pointed out quietly.

The last time had been by accident. This was by design. "I'm asking now."

The exquisite rush began before Brandon ever took her in his arms. Before he even lowered his mouth to hers.

Anticipation could stir up the blood to incredible heights. At times, she was aware, anticipation could lead to disappointment, but not this time. She already knew that.

Knew that the man's kiss was like being bathed in a shower of sparklers.

Her eyes on his, Isabelle murmured, "Permission to come aboard granted," just loud enough for him to hear above the sound of the ocean.

He grinned as he drew her to him, his body heat reaching out to hers.

"Doesn't that have something to do with boarding a ship?" he asked, amused.

"Whatever."

Isabelle was aware that the word sounded utterly lame, but it was the only comeback she could manage right now. Her brain had moved passed conversations and was already otherwise engaged as she rose up on her toes and slid her arms around his neck.

Brandon touched his lips to hers. Very slowly, he lifted her off the sand and folded her into the kiss that was already, even now, claiming his soul as well.

Chapter Eleven

She'd always been an old movie buff, and the classic scene *From Here To Eternity,* of two lovers lying on the beach lost in one another's embrace and kissing, flashed through Isabelle's brain just before she lost the ability to form coherent thoughts. How could one kiss do that? How could it just make the entire world go away?

She hadn't the energy to even *attempt* to figure that out. All she wanted to do was enjoy this moment, this sensation, before it—and possibly she—disappeared forever.

Brandon knew, *knew,* he shouldn't be doing this. Shouldn't be giving in to his urges. The urges might be basic, but Isabelle was his mother's physical therapist, and if things between them went awry, life could become very awkward....

But what if they didn't?

What if things didn't go awry or veer off the track?

Then living with Isabelle just down the hall, seeing her each day, interacting with her, could only be a plus. After all, at its longest this interlude would probably only be for a little less than three more weeks.

Three more weeks and his mother intended to be completely recovered because she had every intention of going on that tour with the rest of the cast of *A Little Night Music*. Knowing his mother, the woman was stubborn enough to *will* herself fit enough to go on tour. With Anastasia away, the dynamics of his household would go back to what they'd been before the accident. Just Victoria and him and, once every two weeks, the cleaning crew that put the house back into order.

That would be life as he knew it. Life as he enjoyed it.

So why shouldn't he allow himself to savor this surprisingly exquisite, unselfconsciously seductive woman while he could? Their paths would stop crossing very soon.

The situation was perfect.

As was this palpable chemistry that had been generated between them.

His arms tightened around Isabelle even more, as if he were trying to absorb her—because, maybe, just for this moment, he was. Absorb her enthusiasm and her very exuberant essence. And this incredible—and unusual—spectrum of happiness she brought out in him.

Isabelle could feel her head spinning, and her body had stopped whispering its demands and was now all but screaming them. With all this work in the past six months or so, she'd almost forgotten she was a female. A woman. And, since she was living and breathing, she did have certain needs. Needs that hadn't really ever been addressed.

Her body now reminded her that its education had been sadly neglected. She didn't intend for that pitiable state to continue a second longer.

This strange, all-but-consuming hunger threatened to swallow her up whole unless she did something about it.

Isabelle pressed her body into his, holding on to Brandon so tightly she was surprised he could still breathe. She certainly was having difficulty getting air in. As she shifted, she took the opportunity to press against him even more urgently, fitting her soft curves against his hard contours.

She felt his response immediately.

Her mouth curved beneath his. The next moment, she was kissing him even more passionately, stealing away the last of his breath. Sacrificing hers as well.

Brandon drew back his head. Breaking contact came under the heading of one of the hardest things he'd had to do. But it had to be done on the very slim, outside chance that Isabelle didn't realize she was about to push him entirely over the edge, emulsifying the last of his control.

"You keep doing that and I'm not going to be responsible for what happens next," he informed her hoarsely.

There was no other way to describe it. The grin that curved her lips in response to his warning was nothing short of wicked.

It placed her in a completely different light in his eyes.

"Doing what?" she murmured innocently, her breath warm and teasing on his lips.

"Kissing me mindless." The answer was tendered with effort. He struggled to hold himself in check when all he wanted to do was lose himself in her, to make love with her until he could no longer move.

She placed a hand to his chest, her fingers lightly feathering along the hard ridges.

Isabelle smiled up into his eyes. "I doubt if anything could render you into a mindless state."

Now there she was wrong. "Keep kissing me like that and you'll find out," he promised.

Laughter entered her eyes. "A challenge. I love a challenge," she whispered huskily.

The next moment, she was kissing him again. Or was that him, kissing her? Brandon wasn't sure. All he knew was that she'd lit a fire within him. A fire that gave no indication that it could be quenched in the near future.

He wanted to take her now, here, in this place, while desire ravaged his body. But this was a public beach, and although the public appeared to be either asleep or elsewhere, he wasn't about to take a chance that one of Newport Beach's finest would somehow show up next to them at the worst possible, inopportune moment.

Besides, he didn't want to take a chance on having Isabelle vulnerable like that.

Aside from the fact that it would be absolutely embarrassing for her, he was fairly certain that he would never hear the end of it from his mother. Not to mention that inevitably, the media would get hold of it and that would embarrass not just Isabelle but his daughter as well. He couldn't risk it.

They needed to go somewhere private. Somewhere there wasn't a chance that his mother would materialize like an apparition who had lost her way.

That meant that his house was out. Granted, he had a

lot of rooms, but they were rooms his mother was given to roaming through at will. They needed somewhere more private.

For the second time in less than five minutes, he forced himself to draw back from the woman who had begun a fire in his core. His voice barely above a hoarse whisper, he said, "We'd better be getting back."

She didn't want to let go of the moment or of the man. But she couldn't very well do what every fiber of her being was begging her to do—at least, not out here, out in the open, no matter how romantic the notion of making love beneath the stars might sound.

She thought of his house. It was huge, but there was always the chance of being interrupted by Anastasia or, far worse, by Victoria.

And then it came to her.

"Would you like to stop at my place…for a night cap?" Isabelle asked, adding the coda just in case he'd suddenly thought better of what he'd just begun and turned her down. It was a way to save face in what could be a dicey situation.

One look into his eyes, and she knew that he wouldn't be turning her down.

"A nightcap sounds good," he told her. *Making love with you sounds better.*

Linking his hand with hers, he stooped down to pick up her shoes with his other hand. They started walking again and made their way back to the bookstore's parking lot.

The bookstore was dark, and the lot was empty except for his car. Aiming his remote at the vehicle, Brandon heard a tiny squeak in response, followed by both locks springing open.

He held the door for her. When Isabelle was seated, he rounded the hood and got in on the driver's side.

Chivalry, she thought with a small, appreciative smile, was not dead. It was alive and well within this dynamically handsome author of thrillers.

His genre was aptly named, she couldn't help thinking, because right at this moment, a thrill ran up and down her spine, ushered in by wave after wave of anticipation.

Every single nerve ending she possessed was at attention right now.

On edge.

Aside from a couple of "almost" experiences in college, both of which ended rather poorly, she had never actually made love with a man before. She was both excited about what lay ahead—and self-consciously worried about it at the same time. What if she didn't measure up?

What if making love with a novice, a virgin, completely turned him off? Being a virgin had never bothered her before. There'd never been anyone to whom she'd wanted to surrender herself to before. But now...

Now she wondered if she'd disappoint him.

Of course she would, she thought, mocking herself. At this point it was only a matter of by how much, not "if." For the first time in her life, she regretted her lack of experience.

There had to be something she could do in order not to disappoint him, she thought frantically.

As they pulled up into her apartment complex, she continued to be both excited and afraid. What if she'd built this up too much? What if he was the one who failed to measure up?

Not possible. Look at him. The man is incapable of

disappointing you, even if he just spends the evening kissing you.

Okay, then, what do I do if I disappoint him?

She had no answer for that one.

Brandon stopped the car but remained seated for a beat longer. Her fingertips began to grow cold. Had he changed his mind? Was he rethinking the situation and finding her to be off-puttingly eager? Or did he feel she was lacking in some way?

Did he suspect that this would be her first time?

Nerves warred within her as she forced words to her ultradry lips. "Something wrong?"

He took a breath. This wasn't easy for him. He'd never been with anyone like Isabelle before. His tastes usually ran toward far more superficial women.

"I don't want you to think that you have to go through with this. What I mean is that I don't want you to feel like you're being pressured to…"

Her. He was thinking of her. Her eyes widened as the last of her solid form melted in the face of his thoughtfulness. With the transmission shift between them, she leaned over, grabbed Brandon by the lapels on his jacket and pressed her lips against his. This time there was no working up to it. This time she was kissing him from the depths of her soul right from the start.

An eternity later, she finally drew back. She needed to come up for air, and it was either that or keel over from lack of oxygen.

"Does that feel like I think I'm being pressured?" Isabelle asked him in a voice that was hardly louder than a whisper.

The smile in his eyes turned to a grin when it reached his lips. "Nope."

She drew a breath, desperately trying to steady her

erratic pulse. "All right, then," was all she said. The next moment, she opened the passenger door and swung her legs out.

She didn't remember walking the short distance from his car to her door. Didn't remember unlocking her door. What she did remember was being caught up in a whirlwind that swept over her the instant they were both inside the apartment. A whirlwind that fed a frenzy shared by both of them.

Hands were everywhere.

His.

Hers.

Hands, touching, claiming. Worshipping. And undressing.

Not slowly and languidly to heighten the intensity by increments but wildly, feeding the fire, stoking the need until it was all-consuming, imprisoning both of them in its ring of flames.

She remembered the feel of his mouth, his lips, his tongue. On her lips, her throat, her skin. Felt their hot imprint on her breasts, her belly.

Everywhere.

She felt the fireworks, the explosions as they rocked her, weakening her. Making her stronger. Bolder. What happened to her now was so much more intense, so much stronger than anything she could have possibly imagined.

She wanted to laugh, to cry, to scream with joy. Above all else, she didn't want this exhilarating experience to end.

Ever.

He'd never had a partner react the way she did. Had never felt the need to keep increasing a partner's plea-sure the way he desperately wanted to heighten hers. It was like unwrapping layer after layer of a gift only to find more layers waiting for him.

Excitement coursed through his veins, and it was almost like making love for the first time. Not a first time with a new partner but for the very first time. *Ever.*

Because of her reactions, her eagerness, the way she twisted into him, the way she caressed him, at first almost timidly, then eagerly and finally, wantonly, she made everything seem brand-new and fresh again.

Made him want to do it all and see it through her eyes to increase his own pleasure even as he sought to cull hers.

Eternity seemed nestled within each heartbeat. The more he did, the more he wanted to do. As incredible as it seemed to him in hindsight, he just could not get enough of her. She made him insatiable.

But finally, unable to hold himself in check a second longer, Brandon knew it was time for the song that had been playing so wildly between them to reach its highest crescendo.

Holding her hands above her head, lacing his fingers through hers, he joined their mouths together a moment before he began to move himself into her. He heard the small gasp that escaped her lips. Or rather, he *tasted* it.

The resistance he met surprised him. It never occurred to him that she was—

His eyes widened. But before he could draw back, before he could ask, she was wrapping her legs around his, pulling him in. Forcing him forward.

He *felt* her cry as it emerged and then echoed between them. The next moment, she was moving her hips, enticing him.

Sealing the last outstanding bond between them, they were now truly one.

He began to move first slowly then, as she responded, more and more quickly until they were both breathlessly racing to an invisible goal line that was just beyond their reach.

And then it wasn't.

It was theirs.

His fingers tightened around hers just at the moment of release, and he could have sworn he heard her crying out his name.

A shower of fireworks and glimmering stars rained over them, euphoria grasping both of them and clutching tightly before slowly releasing its hold by inches.

He wanted to stay like this indefinitely, but he knew he couldn't keep his weight off her for long, no matter how good his intentions were. Besides, he had to know if he was right.

Pivoting on his elbows, Brandon drew back, separating their physical union but not their souls. One hand around her, he moved Isabelle closer to him.

Slowly, his surroundings began to dawn on him. They were on the floor in her living room, clothes scattered on either side of them. The coffee table had gotten kicked to one side.

He had no memory of that. No memory of anything, really, except for the hunger that had taken bites out of the pit of his stomach because he'd wanted her so much.

"Isabelle?"

Here it came, she thought, tensing. The question. Had he been greatly disappointed or only just a little?

"Yes?" she murmured so quietly, he almost didn't hear her.

"Are you..." He had trouble forming the word, because with it came guilt. "A virgin?"

"Not anymore." She deliberately avoided his eyes, looking off to the side.

"But you were."

"We all were at one point or other."

"Don't play games with me."

She couldn't remember ever hearing him sound this stern before. "Yes," she admitted. "I'm sorry."

The words he was about to say froze as he looked at her, utterly confused. "Sorry?" he echoed. "Why are you sorry?"

"That I obviously disappointed you."

He drew himself up a little more, staring down at her incredulously. "Where did you get that idea?"

"Then I didn't disappoint you?" she asked, surprised.

"No," he said emphatically. "Of course not. But if you'd told me ahead of time, I would have gone slower, been more gentle...."

"Not possible," she answered. "You were perfect. And if I'd have told you, you wouldn't have made love with me," she pointed out. "Would you?"

She had him there. But not for the reason she thought. "No, I wouldn't have," he admitted. "But only because a girl's first time should be something special, with someone special."

Her eyes held his. "What makes you think it wasn't?"

He didn't know how to answer that. How to share the warm feeling her words had just created within him. So he changed the subject. Sort of.

Looking around, he observed, "I guess we never made it to the bedroom."

Relieved that he'd dropped the matter of her virginity,

she smiled. "Guess not. Next time," she said. The next moment, her own words replayed themselves in her head and she tried to backtrack. "I mean..."

He saw the slight embarrassment, saw the splash of color coming into her cheeks. Why did that make her look so appealingly adorable? He didn't even like the color pink.

"Next time," he echoed, coming to her rescue.

He was rewarded with a grateful smile and knew he'd instinctively said the right thing.

Pressing a kiss to her forehead, more tender than heated, he said, "Give me a few minutes to catch my breath and we can see about making this time the 'next time.'"

Amazed, she propped herself up on her elbow and looked at him. Everything she'd ever heard pointed to most men only being interested in one thing, and when it was over, they went on their way—or fell asleep.

"Really?"

He could only smile in response as the words "delightful" and "adorable" echoed in his head again.

"Really," he said, not a hundred percent sure what he'd just confirmed, knowing only that it seemed to make her happy, and he'd discovered that he enjoyed doing that. Enjoyed it a great deal.

It had been a long time since he'd felt this free, this content. It came as a double surprise because he'd been convinced that his distrust of his own reactions would always mar the experience for him. He had Jean to thank for that.

And now, for however long this lasted, he had Isabelle to thank for bringing him back from that numb, dark place.

Chapter Twelve

"You were very late getting in last night," Anastasia commented to Isabelle during the following morning's physical therapy session. Because she was fairly certain that she looked a little unnerved at the observation, she wasn't surprised to hear the actress explain, "I was having one of my sleepless nights and for once, the book I was reading did *not* put me to sleep. I had my bedroom door partially opened and I heard the two of you when you came in."

Isabelle instinctively braced herself for a volley of questions. It was an ingrained response. When she'd lived at home, her father would always grill her, bombarding her with questions whenever she came home after a date. At first she'd told herself it was just because he cared and was being overly protective. Eventually she realized it was because he was jealous that she was paying attention to another male. Though he never displayed any affection toward her, he wanted to be the focus of her world. He never seemed to understand that in order to get so much, he needed to give at least a little.

Braced, she was more than a little relieved when all Anastasia asked was, "Did you have a good time?"

The woman seemed apparently satisfied with the answer she gave when she said, "Yes."

Resuming the new task she'd been assigned involving a large, colorful scarf that was tied around her upper thighs and keeping it there as she moved across the room, Anastasia smiled and nodded quickly.

"Good. About time my son saw the value of the company of a decent young woman." She rolled her eyes as she confided, "You should have seen who he's taken out in the past. They all looked like special deliveries directly from some upscale cathouse. And not a single one of them would drown in a flash flood even if they wanted to, if you know what I mean." She gave Isabelle a penetrating look.

She knew exactly what Anastasia meant. That the women Brandon Slade went out with were all well-endowed—or at least well-enhanced.

In that kind of inflated company, she was definitely someone who could be overlooked or lost in the shuffle when it came to large cup sizes, Isabelle thought.

"Not one of them has the IQ of an intelligent shoe-lace," Anastasia lamented. She shook her head. "I have no idea what he sees in them—beyond the obvious, of course." She shook her head as she continued to attempt to walk without allowing the scarf to drop. "He has better standards than that."

Maybe he didn't, Isabelle couldn't help thinking. "I don't think your son's end goal is to really be *mentally* stimulated," Isabelle pointed out. But heaven knew that the word "stimulated" was dead on in this case. Forcing her mind back on Anastasia, she frowned. "And you've stopped moving," she told the actress in as stern a voice as she could manage. She glanced at her wristwatch. "C'mon, you've only got ten more minutes to go."

Anastasia scowled. She looked down at the scarf, which had slipped several inches and was in danger of pooling down to the floor altogether. Keeping it up was a combined effort of the muscles in her thighs and sheer determination. The exercise, one that Isabelle had created herself, had her moving from one end of the gym to the other, waddling in effect, while keeping the multicolored scarf in place.

So far, the actress was having only moderate success. Each time the scarf sank past her knees, the event was accompanied by more than a few choice words hurled at the world of physical therapy in general.

As before, several steps later, the scarf had sunk down, this time encircling Anastasia's ankles and threatening to make her trip.

The woman lost her legendary temper. "What is the godforsaken *point* of all this ridiculous nonsense?" she thundered in a voice that she usually used to project to the very last seat in a large theater—without the aid of a microphone.

Isabelle bent down and retrieved the scarf, once again slipping it back into place for the actress.

"In an odd sort of way, the point is the same as learning to walk with a book balanced on your head. One is to perfect your posture and keep your back erect and strong, the other is to strengthen your thighs, especially the one on the leg that's been operated on. Both boil down to a matter of extreme complete control."

Anastasia looked unconvinced. "You're just trying to change the subject," she sniffed.

No, she didn't want to discuss the subject, Isabelle thought. What had happened was between Brandon and her. Last night had been special, and she had tucked it away, out of the light of day, where it would remain.

Right now, what she wanted to do was to concentrate on the reason she'd been hired in the first place. To rehabilitate Anastasia in time to join the tour before it left Los Angeles.

She pinned Anastasia with a look that was meant to convey to the woman that she meant business. It was a look she'd seen her mother give her father often enough when she was growing up. Back then, there'd been frost attached to it.

"As far as I'm concerned, Anastasia, you *are* the subject."

It was obvious that, although it was usually second nature to the woman, this time the actress didn't want to focus on herself. At least, not yet. "Be that as it may, I want to know if you two *really* enjoyed yourselves."

She knew. For a self-absorbed woman, Anastasia certainly did pick up on things in her surroundings, Isabella thought.

"I can't speak for your son, but yes, I had a very nice time at the reception," she said evasively.

"And afterward?" Anastasia asked shrewdly.

"Afterward was nice, too," Isabelle allowed, trying not to smile too much. This much she could tell the woman, she thought.

Anything more was either admitting too much or taking something for granted. That part was up to him to admit or deny. She didn't want to get ahead of herself—or get carried away. With her father as a glaring example, she was well aware that acute disappointments lay in that direction. She would far rather just go along the way she was than get her hopes up, only to see them come crashing down around her in shattered, painful fragments.

Besides, if things went sour with Brandon while she was still here working with Anastasia, at the very least it would make working conditions awkward for her. At the worst, it would make them intolerable. She was not about to do anything to set those kinds of waves in motion.

Better to have nothing than to have something blow up on you.

To her surprise, Brandon's mother didn't press any more. The woman gave her a completely inscrutable smile, murmured, "I see," and then terminated any line of further questioning.

Isabelle didn't know whether to be highly relieved— or very suspicious. From everything she'd ever read about the dynamic actress, Anastasia Del Vecchio was not the type who subscribed to the "let sleeping dogs lie" philosophy. On the contrary, she was the kind of person who insisted on always being in the know and in the thick of things.

What was she up to?

Again, Isabelle forced herself to focus on the exercise at hand. She tapped her watch. "You still have nine more minutes to go, you know."

"No, I don't," Anastasia protested. She swept her hand majestically toward the south wall and pointed to the clock. "Eight minutes have gone by since you said I had ten to go."

"Ten *working* minutes," Isabelle emphasized. "Not talking minutes."

Anastasia pouted. "Anyone named 'Legree' in your family tree?" she asked. "As in Simon Leree? He was the evil plantation—"

"I know where the reference comes from, Anastasia," Isabelle replied patiently. Humoring the woman, she answered, "And no, there's no one with that surname in my family tree. Not to mention the fact that he was fictional."

Anastasia smiled despite her impatience to get the exercise over with. The fact that Isabelle was familiar with a book written in the mid 1800s was, to her, a testament to the young woman being well-read and well-rounded. That made her all the more perfect for Brandon. There had to be some subtle way to make him see that.

But not too subtle, Anastasia silently emphasized. For the most part, too much subtlety was lost on men, her son included.

She decided to work a little on Isabelle. Surely the young woman wouldn't object to a few honest questions. "But you do find my son attractive?"

The question ended on a note that implied she was waiting for nothing short of a positive answer. Isabelle debated whether it was worth the effort to tell the woman that this was not exactly the sort of subject that should be discussed, seeing as how Brandon was her son. It probably wasn't worth the effort, she decided, and gave the only answer possible, since she had twenty-twenty vision.

"Yes, I find him attractive." What woman in her right mind wouldn't? His face was the stuff of dreams. Erotic dreams, she amended. "I would have to be blind not to."

Anastasia bestowed an almost beatific smile on her. "He needs a good woman, you know."

No, she didn't know. And neither did Brandon, she was willing to bet. From the articles she'd read about him before she'd met him, Brandon seemed very happy with having a different woman on his arm for each occasion. Yesterday, it had been her. Tomorrow, it would be someone else.

Why that made her stomach into a knot she wouldn't even explore. She'd known all this before she'd gone to bed with him. Before she even accepted the job. It was just the way that things were.

Out loud she said, "He seems very happy with his present lifestyle. Don't turn your right leg out that far," she coached. "You want to keep your gait equal to give your left leg enough time to catch up properly."

"He isn't, you know. Happy with his present lifestyle," Anastasia explained when Isabelle looked at her quizzically. "Brandon's the marrying kind. Unlike me, for him marriage was supposed to last forever. Part of him is still in shock dating back to when Victoria's mother, Jean, walked out on him. Brandon had to beg her to have Victoria, you know," she added, her voice dropping to a conspiratorial whisper in case her granddaughter picked this moment to walk in. "Jean wanted to terminate her pregnancy the minute she knew for certain that she was expecting."

No, she didn't know that. It wasn't any of her business to know, Isabelle thought. But even so, the knowledge of that one not-so-small fact, that Brandon had wanted his daughter from the moment she came into existence, made her heart open up a little more toward the man.

No longer even pretending to work her exercise, an immobile Anastasia shook her head. "Poor guy thought that when Jean held the baby in her arms, she'd come around. Well, she didn't and I say he's the luckier for it because she took her self-centered behind and ran off when Victoria was less than a month old.

"She did try to come back," Anastasia told her, lowering her voice in case it carried. "Right after Brandon hit the *New York Times* bestseller list for the first time. He almost, almost forgave her, too," the actress lamented. And then she smiled. "Until he realized that she didn't think she'd done anything wrong. That and the private investigator's report made up his mind for him and he turned her away."

"Private investigator's report?" Isabelle echoed, waiting for more details.

Anastasia nodded, looking very smug and pleased with herself. "I hired one to look into what my ex-daughter-in-law had been up to since she'd last darkened Brandon's door. Quite the promiscuous little party girl, Jean was. Still is, probably."

"Mother, you have to have more recent stories than that to entertain your physical therapist with."

Both women nearly jumped, startled. Brandon stood in the gym's doorway, having entered silently behind them.

With a dramatic intake of breath, Anastasia splayed a very heavily jeweled hand across her ample chest. "You shouldn't sneak up on me like that, Brandon. You could have given me a heart attack," she declared. Then her eyes narrowed ever so slightly. "How long have you been standing there?

"You know you don't get heart attacks, Mother. You give them," he told her with a knowing smile. "And as for how long I've been standing here listening, I'll just leave that up to your fertile imagination."

Indignant, Anastasia chided her son. "Brandon, you shouldn't eavesdrop."

"I wasn't eavesdropping," he countered. "I came by to ask Isabelle if she had plans for dinner tonight."

"Oh, wait, I think I hear Victoria calling me," Anastasia announced. She looked from Isabelle to him before continuing. "I'd better go and see what she wants."

"Victoria must have a more powerful voice than I thought. She's down the street, at Marisol's house," Brandon said, doing his best to suppress a smile. He only partially succeeded. "That's her best friend," he said for Isabelle's benefit.

"I know. She told me," Isabelle replied.

Somewhat shy at first, Brandon's daughter had taken to her rather quickly, a fact that pleased her a great deal. She found the young girl refreshingly devoid of all the stereotypical angst and hang-ups associated with most girls her age. The twelve-year-old was really more of a young adult than an adolescent. In a way, Victoria reminded her a lot of herself.

Anastasia refused to be caught in a lie, even if everyone already knew that it was. This was no exception. "Still, I'd better go and check. I'm absolutely certain I just heard her." Placing a hand on her son's arm for balance, she shimmied the scarf off her thighs and gracefully stepped out of the bright, colorful circle. Finally regaining her mobility, the actress nodded at the scarf on the floor. "Be a dear and pick that up for Isabelle, will you, Brandon?"

With that, the woman swept out of the room, as regal as any queen.

"Your wish is my command, Mother," he murmured good-naturedly, bending over to pick up the scarf. Straightening, he offered it back to Isabelle. "I'll say one thing for my mother. She is nothing if not dramatically colorful."

"I heard that." Anastasia's voice echoed back into the room despite the fact that she was no longer in his line of sight.

Seeming to address Isabelle, he raised his voice so that it would carry. "Among other things she has in common with the nocturnal creatures, she also has the hearing of a bat."

This time, his mother prudently said nothing. There was no way she was about to acknowledge his very flippant remark.

Isabelle's curiosity was getting the better of her. She supposed she could pretend that he hadn't initially said anything, but then she might miss out on being with him again. And fleeting though it would, right now she didn't want to pass up a single opportunity to spend some time with Brandon.

"You said something about dinner?" she prodded, even as part of her wondered if she really should. She didn't want to seem too eager. But then again, she was afraid if she remained too passive, he'd just move on that much sooner.

Brandon nodded, getting back to his initial question. "Right. I promised my friend I'd give his new restaurant a try and my date just canceled on me at the last minute. I hate eating by myself in public, so I was wondering if you were available."

His date had canceled at the last minute.

He had a date. With another woman. After they'd made love together last night.

Talk about a fast operator...

Well of course he has a date. He didn't exactly pledge his undying love and loyalty last night, now did he? And for the record, neither did you.

Just take it for what it was, a wonderful evening with an extremely desirable man.

Okay, so it wasn't a wonderful evening, it was the best evening of her whole life, but that was no reason to lose sight of reality. Their time together had been special, unique. *Not* the start of something big.

"Sure. If you can't find anyone else to go," she added, deliberately giving him a way out if his first choice called back.

Brandon picked up on it immediately. He detected a definite lack of enthusiasm in Isabelle's voice and manner. And he had a sneaking feeling he knew why.

He'd worded things better in his life, Brandon thought, upbraiding himself.

"I didn't look for anyone else," he told her. "And that date that canceled—"

She raised her hand as if to physically stop the flow of words. "Wait. Brandon. I'm sorry if I made you think that—well, you don't owe me an explanation—"

This time it was his turn to interrupt her. "I know, I was volunteering information. I just wanted you to know that I made that date two months ago, when my friend gave me the opening date for his restaurant. I didn't even know you then."

There was no reason for her to feel that burst of sunshine going off inside of her. After all, she *knew* this was just temporary and had just spent the morning telling herself over and over again that she wasn't expecting anything lasting from him.

And truth be told, if she suspected their friendship *could* last, she'd already be packing up and heading for the hills.

Because something like that, something that promised to be lasting, that promised her love for a lifetime, had disaster and heartache written all over it in big, bold neon letters.

Even though she knew how she would react, and still, still she couldn't help herself. Right now, in this very moment in time, she just couldn't stop smiling.

As if she actually believed in love and "happily ever after."

She *knew* better than that.

Isabelle kept on smiling anyway.

Chapter Thirteen

"Are you sure you want to do this?"

Brandon sat on Victoria's canopied double bed, watching his daughter debating between which pair of almost identical white cutoffs to take with her to summer camp.

Was it his imagination, or were there fewer stuffed animals lining the bottom shelf of her bookcase in her ultrafeminine bedroom than usual?

It was official. His daughter was growing up much too fast.

Victoria never broke stride. She was only half packed and her best friend's mother was coming by soon to pick her up to drive them to the camp bus. She'd been adamant about her father not coming along. She didn't think he was up to watching her board the bus.

"Dad, I'm all packed and you paid for my two weeks

at camp way back in April. It's nonrefundable," she reminded him.

Money was so not the point here. He was finally at a stage in his life where money no longer represented a concern of any kind.

He shook his head. "Doesn't matter. If you're having second thoughts or cold feet about going, don't feel as if you have to leave," he told her.

Victoria paused to smile at him fondly. "My feet are as warm as the rest of me, Dad. I *want* to go. It'll be fun," she promised him encouragingly. She crossed to the bureau to check if she'd left anything behind on the list she'd made for herself.

Victoria might not be having second thoughts, but he was. He liked having his daughter around, and this was her first time away from home. Victoria was well-traveled, but they had always done it together.

"All right," he allowed reluctantly, "but if you get there and decide you want to come home—"

She closed her eyes and answered him, reciting the words as if they'd been drummed into her head. "I'll call you to come rescue me."

"Right." Well, at least he'd gotten that across to her.

After his daughter crossed back to the bed, she deposited three more items into the suitcase, then snapped the locks into place. This was it. She was really going. With a sigh, he got off the bed.

"You have your cell phone?"

"In my pocket, Dad." She tapped the slight bulge in the pocket of her candy-striped shorts.

Brandon nodded, casting about for a way to stall and squeeze out an extra minute or two longer with his daughter. "Good. And your charger? You didn't forget your charger, did you?"

"In my suitcase," she answered patiently. "Next to the whistle you gave me to blow in case I see a snake charging at me."

He'd have to be deaf to miss what the tone in her voice was saying. "Okay, maybe I'm being a little over-protective—" he allowed.

Victoria flashed him a very knowing, tolerant grin. "You think?"

Taking her suitcase off the bed for her, he slung his free arm around her shoulders as they made their way out of the room. "But you're the only daughter I have and it would be such a pain breaking in a brand-new one. Try to come back in one piece for me, okay?"

She pretended to take that as a serious request. "I'll do my best, Dad." And then, as they came to the top of the stairs, she looked at him and softened. "It's going to be okay," she told him as if she was the parent and he the child who needed reassuring.

"Yeah, I know," he said, so proud of her it hurt.

They went down the stairs. Anastasia deliberately let them have a moment together and waited in another room until she could say goodbye.

Brandon turned toward his daughter as she reached the bottom step. "Victoria?"

She checked her purse one last time for the new essentials in her life: light pink lipstick and suntan lotion. "Yes, Dad?"

"You don't think I've been an unavailable father, do you?"

Victoria glanced up from her search, snapping her purse closed. She did her best not to laugh. "Dad, if you were any more available, I'd have to run away from home."

He saw a very real parallel in her reply. "Is that why you're...?"

Because she was his daughter, she knew where this was going. They had a very strong bond and often had the same thoughts.

"No! Dad, you're the best dad in the whole world. I'm a really lucky kid. You've always been there for me and I've never felt the lack of anything. I have no complaints. Except—"

"Aha, you *do* have a complaint." Here it came. He braced himself.

When she spoke, she didn't say anything remotely close to what he was expecting. "I think you need a girlfriend."

Stunned, he stared at her. "What?"

Victoria explained patiently, "Dad, you're not getting any younger and neither am I. I'm going to start dating, going away to college. You need another hobby other than me." She sighed and gazed at him. "How about Isabelle? She seems very nice. Gemma likes her and you know how hard *she* is to please. And I think Isabelle's great."

Just then, a car horn beeped three times, then twice. Victoria grabbed her suitcase. "That's Marisol's mom. I've gotta go. Tell me you'll at least think about what I just said," she implored.

He didn't want to think about it. Didn't want to think about Victoria dating or going away to college. It was hard enough for him to let her go for a sleepover for a single night, much less a semester...or even longer. But for her peace of mind, he murmured dutifully, "I'll think about it."

Victoria rose up on her toes and brushed a quick kiss to his cheek. "Thanks. Now, you're not going to worry, right?"

"Right," he muttered, his heart clearly not in the lie he was parroting back.

In a rare display of sensitivity, Anastasia had deliberately remained out of sight in order to give her son and granddaughter time together. But now, as if right on cue, the actress swept into the foyer, her electric blue caftan billowing about her, and encircled her granddaughter with her arms to give her a huge hug.

"Have a good time, Victoria. Learn a craft for me," she instructed.

Victoria flashed a grin at her grandmother as she extricated herself from the hug. "Will do, Gemma," she promised.

Isabelle had been hovering just within the family room, waiting until Brandon and Anastasia were finished. She didn't want to interrupt a family moment, but she didn't want to miss an opportunity to say goodbye to the young girl, or to tell her to have fun.

Not that, Isabelle judged, she needed instruction for that. Victoria, an obvious product of her father's loving care and understanding, was the most levelheaded young person she had ever encountered. Love did that, she thought. Made a person strong and able to face anything.

In a way, she envied Victoria her secure upbringing.

"Have fun, Victoria," Isabelle said, joining the small circle.

"I will!" Victoria responded with enthusiasm, eager to get going. Impulsively, she threw her arms around

Isabelle and took the opportunity to whisper into her ear, "Take care of Dad for me."

Surprised by the request, Isabelle drew back and looked at Brandon's daughter. "I will."

The answer came out automatically because taking care of people was both her vocation and her mission in life. A beat later, she realized how that must have sounded and hoped that Brandon hadn't heard what Victoria had said to her.

"Would it offend your independent sensibilities if I carried your suitcase to the car?" Brandon asked her.

Victoria pretended that granting permission was a huge concession on her part. "I suppose so." Her mouth curved, giving her away.

Father and daughter went out the door. To Isabelle's surprise, Anastasia made no attempt to follow. She remained in the foyer. Her sniffling drew Isabelle's attention back to her.

"Why is there never a tissue around when you need one?" Anastasia demanded, annoyed.

Isabelle dug into her pocket and produced a small packet of tissues and silently passed it to the woman.

Taking the packet, Anastasia sniffled again. "Should have known you'd be like a Girl Scout. Always prepared." She made the pronouncement almost longingly, as if she thought self-sufficiency had its appeal.

"I think those are the Boy Scouts," Isabelle corrected gently.

"We're not supposed to discriminate these days," Anastasia replied, waving a hand in wide, concentric circles in the air. She blew her nose, then wadded up the tissue. Looking just a tad uncertain, she slanted a glance in Isabelle's direction. "Victoria'll be all right, won't she?"

Isabelle was surprised the woman asked her that question. Anastasia Del Vecchio always projected such a strong, confident image on and off the screen. Seeing this vulnerable, uncertain side to the woman took her aback. It also, Isabelle thought, made the woman exceedingly human in her eyes.

"I think that, interestingly enough, out of the three of you, Victoria's the one who is the most 'all right.'" The look in Anastasia's eyes told her that the woman struggled very hard not to cry. *Very human,* Isabelle thought. "You and your son did a great job raising her. She's mature and secure and very, very levelheaded. More than I was at her age."

Anastasia was instantly her old self, waving away the assessment. "Oh, I sincerely doubt that, Isabelle. I think you were born old."

Isabelle examined the comment. "I'm not sure if that's a compliment," she said, bemused.

Over the past few weeks, Anastasia had grown exceedingly fond of her physical therapist. Setting aside her bombastic persona for a moment, she took Isabelle's hand in hers and patted it.

"It was meant as one, dear." Releasing her hand again, she glanced back toward the room she'd been in. "Well, I think I'll go lie down and absorb all this. Saying goodbye has taken a lot out of me."

Isabelle smiled to herself. The drama queen had returned. In this case, it was a good sign.

"Fine. I think we're about done for the day, anyway." She regarded the woman warmly. "You deserve some time off for good behavior."

"You're only saying that because you want to get ready for your night out," the actress responded intuitively, giving her a knowing look.

"Well, having more than five minutes to throw on a dress and put my makeup on would be nice, yes," Isabelle agreed.

Anastasia paused to regard her for a moment, as if to scrutinize her more closely.

"Oh, my dear, you're still so very young—don't you know you don't need any help?" As she said the words, there was a note of longing in the actress's voice for the years that had gone by.

There were times when she felt old and other times when she felt invisible. Now was not the time to argue about either. "I guess I am young at that," Isabelle agreed, then winked playfully at Anastasia. "Almost as young as you are."

Anastasia laughed. She knew that Isabelle was neither pandering to her ego, nor being sarcastic. Her words were tendered with affection. As a rule, the actress did not like many women, feeling, instead a sharp sense of competition whenever she was in the company of another female. Such was not the case with Isabelle. She genuinely liked her.

Moreover, she hoped that Brandon would have the good sense to snap her up before some other man did.

"You'll do, Isabelle Sinclair," the actress told her, not bothering to appear regally austere, an image she ordinarily projected for the benefit of those outside the parameters of her own family. "You'll do."

Just as Anastasia left the foyer, Isabelle heard the front door behind her open and close again. Turning around, she saw Brandon standing just inside the doorway. In her opinion, the writer had looked a lot happier than he did right at this moment.

Casting about for something comforting to say, she

waited for him to speak first. She didn't want to intrude into his private moment.

Brandon sighed deeply as he shoved his hands into his pockets. "Well, she's gone."

"She's going to have a wonderful time, Brandon," Isabelle assured him. "Someone with Victoria's level-headedness needs to be able to kick back a little, have some wholesome fun. Otherwise, I have a feeling she might just spend the whole summer reading books and never even venturing outside the house."

"Yeah, I know. You're right. Camp was a good idea. She'll have fun." A small sigh escaped, and he looked as though he had a momentary lapse of control. "She probably won't even miss—home," he said, substituting another word for the one he meant at the last minute.

Not that he fooled her at all. Isabelle struggled not to smile, even though she thought it rather sweet that he was so protective of his daughter. Not for the first time, she thought how lucky Victoria was to have such a relaxed relationship with her father. He was both her friend and her protector. Most of the time, you got either one or the other.

And sometimes, she thought with a pang, as in her case, you got neither.

"I'm sure she'll miss 'home,'" she told him with the proper emphasis on the last word. "But you know, it's also nice to have the opportunity to miss 'home,' instead of always hanging around 'home' and not knowing what a day without being 'home' is like."

By the time she took a breath, it was utterly obvious just what she meant each time she'd said "home." He hadn't really been trying to be subtle when he'd switched his words at the last minute.

Brandon frowned. "Are you through?"

Rather than answer him, she asked, "Do you want to cancel our dinner date?"

He had no idea what one thing had to do with the other. If he lived to be a hundred and twenty, he just *knew* he'd never understand how the female mind worked. "No."

Isabelle smiled, relieved. She really liked the idea of going out with him. To her, this was an unofficial "date." "Then I'm through." She began to walk away and head for the stairs.

He sighed, shaking his head. "I always thought that understanding women would get easier the older I got."

Isabelle stopped and turned around. She was *not* about to put herself out on a limb and assume something. When he said nothing further to follow up on his statement, she prodded, "And?"

"And, I was incredibly wrong," Brandon confessed. "It doesn't get any easier. Matter of fact, it gets harder."

Men were always saying that, she thought. But that was because they liked having their mystery plots complicated and their women simple. It didn't work like that. Smiling, she said, "We're not so hard to understand."

Brandon's eyes narrowed slightly, as if he was trying to fathom the meaning being her words, and then, when he realized she was serious, he laughed.

"Ha!"

Isabelle continued as if he hadn't interjected anything. "We respond to kindness and honesty—and a sense of humor never hurt the situation."

There he begged to differ. "Unless I laugh at a dress you wear."

Isabelle inclined her head. He was right there. She stood corrected. "Unless you laugh at a dress I wear," she agreed. The moment she echoed his phrase, she remembered. "Speaking of which—"

If she didn't get started soon, she wouldn't be ready by the time he'd indicated that he wanted to leave.

"Laughing or dress?" Brandon asked her, a smile curving the corners of his mouth.

"Dress. I have to," she reminded him, ready to race up the stairs.

In place of the easy smile, a seductive, sexy one slipped over his lips as Brandon thought of the way she'd been last night. He couldn't remember if he'd told her how beautiful she was wearing only a sigh. He knew he'd meant to.

"Only if you want to," he told her.

"I want to," she answered with a laugh. Deep down inside, she was flattered by the look in his eyes. Flattered and aroused. "I have no intention of being arrested for nudity and public indecency."

"There was nothing indecent about your nudity," he assured her, sounding so serious when he said it that, just like that, her heart was in serious jeopardy of brimming over.

"Still," she told him as she headed toward the stairs a little more slowly, "I don't think you need that kind of a news-grabbing headline attached to you. It's not exactly the kind of attention the father of a preteen likes to have drawn to him."

She could feel his eyes peeling away the layers of her clothing as he regarded her.

"Oh, I don't know. I might be willing to risk it, given the right woman," he told her with such a straight face, she didn't know if he was being serious or not.

But, whether or not *he* was serious, she had always been the sensible one in any gathering numbering two or more. That being the case again, Isabelle patted his handsome face and declared, "Well, I'm not willing," just before hurrying up the stairs.

She was only halfway up when he called to her, and she stopped again.

"Yes?"

"Thanks."

She could have gotten completely lost in his smile. He *had* to have the most soul-affecting one she'd ever encountered. It took her a moment to locate her brain. "For?"

He was honest with her, something he discovered he could be. Something that hadn't been possible for him with anyone else outside of the two women already in his life. With Isabelle, he could be himself and not worry that she could use it against him, or criticize him. Or laugh when he didn't want her to.

"For pulling me out of a dark place just now," he told her.

"Don't mention it," she told him cheerfully. "It's all included in your mother's bill. It's listed right under 'cheerfulness on demand.' By the way, the first fifty times are free," she added with a wink he found tantalizingly sexy.

His daughter's parting words to him echoed in his head.

"Maybe you were on to something after all, Victoria," he murmured under his breath.

Reaching the top, Isabelle turned around one last time. She thought she heard him say something, but she wasn't entirely sure it wasn't her imagination. "You say something?" she asked.

He looked up at her innocently. "Nope."

Taking the stairs two steps at a time with his long

gait, he would have caught up to her—if she hadn't started running.

Isabelle made it to the guest bedroom before he could make a grab for her.

Her laughter as she eluded him wrapped itself around him, teasing him. Making him yearn at the same time that it made him happy just to be alive.

Chapter Fourteen

"This wasn't a good idea."

Brandon sounded so solemn when he said it, Isabelle braced herself for what didn't want to hear.

She desperately scrambled to sound upbeat, fervently hoping to hold off whatever it was he was going to say to her for a little while longer.

"What wasn't?" she asked brightly, then supplied a benign answer before Brandon could respond. "Dinner out?"

The restaurant had seemed pleasant enough, but nothing about either the decor or the menu set the place apart. It would either require some sort of a makeover with an interesting motif, or a whole host of friends frequenting the premises nightly in order to keep the new restaurant out of the red until it found its identity.

He looked at Isabelle for a second, absorbing her answer. "What? No, that was okay. I'm talking about 'this.'" To underscore his point, he waved one hand about. Then, in case his point still didn't come across, he put a fine point on it. "Dancing."

After they'd had their meal and Brandon had gone to exchange a few words with his friend and wish the man luck with his new venture, she'd impulsively suggested that they go dancing. The restaurant, as it so happened, was only several blocks away from a club where they actually played music that couples could hear and dance to rather than the mind-numbing throbbing which supposedly passed for music in a great many of the more popular clubs.

As she recalled, Brandon had agreed readily enough. There'd been no arm-twisting required on her part, or even anything beyond a suggestion.

Obviously, between that time and now, Brandon had changed his mind.

Why?

She hadn't stepped on his toes. Thanks to her obsessive mother who had sent both Zoe and her for extensive dancing lessons when they were girls, insisting that they needed to "move gracefully, not like wild animals about to attack," Isabelle was fairly certain that she danced well.

So what was it he objected to? Being with her in the first place?

She might as well find out the truth now, she thought, instead of stalling. "I thought you liked dancing."

He looked down into her eyes as he whirled her about the floor to the rhythm of a very seductive blues number. "I do."

Okay, she was officially confused. "Then why don't you think that 'this' was a good idea?"

A half smile curved Brandon's mouth. He would have

thought that was self-evident. "Because holding you in my arms like this and not kissing you is damn harder than I thought it would be."

Oh.

Isabelle breathed an inward sigh of relief and then turned her face up to his. There wasn't even an inch between their bodies. "Who says you can't kiss me?" she challenged.

"Here?" he asked, looking around.

He was obviously a lot more formal than she'd initially thought he was. She found it rather sweet. It also made her bolder.

"Here," she confirmed. "I really don't think anyone is going to notice."

Except for her, she added silently. But that was all good. Besides, maybe it was the wine at dinner, but she really didn't care if anyone *did* notice. She'd come out of her shell. The private Isabelle Sinclair was no longer a shy, quiet, timid creature that all self-respecting church mice were modeled after. These days she caught herself laughing more and admiring the brass ring she'd managed to snare while on this wild merry-go-round ride. It was a ring she knew she was going to have to give back eventually. But not, apparently, just yet.

"Maybe I'll just put your theory to the test," Brandon suggested.

The hand that had been, only a moment ago, pressed to the small of her back now cupped her chin, tilting her face up a little more so that he didn't have so far to lean down for his lips to touch hers. Cover hers. Draw life from hers.

And just like that, her head began spinning. He stole her breath away, leaving her completely, deliciously disoriented. She felt her body hum.

She could easily get addicted to this, Isabelle thought happily.

If she wasn't already.

When she realized that her eyelids had slipped shut, Isabelle forced them opened again.

"Maybe you're right," she conceded. "Dancing with you like this makes me want to do things that have no business being done on a dance floor." Her eyes were almost dancing as she said it.

"At least a crowded dance floor," he amended, feeling the heat from her body reaching out to his.

Why hadn't she noticed how wicked Brandon's grin could get? And how wildly her pulse could beat in response?

Pulling her even closer to him, eliminating the last hint of a space between them, he asked her if she was "Ready to go home?"

"Ready," she breathed, even though she had no idea if he wanted to continue what he'd started just now on the dance floor, or if he was merely making a suggestion that it was time to leave.

All she knew was that she was ready. Ready, with every fiber of her being, to follow this wild, exciting sensation within her to its logical conclusion. When they'd made love last night, Brandon had unlocked something inside of her. Something that had been suppressed all these years. Something that thrilled to the mere hint of his touch, his fingers strumming along her skin as if she was a precious string instrument and he was dedicated to unlocking her secrets.

Leaving the dance floor, they paused by their table just long enough for her to gather her things together. Brandon left a large bill on the table guaranteed to pay for the two drinks they'd ordered plus a heavy tip.

Once outside, Brandon gave his ticket to the valet who in turn promptly ran off to fetch his vehicle. The teen was back within moments. Hopping out, he held the door open for Brandon, then hurried over to help Isabelle into her side of the car.

Brandon left the valet grinning like a Cheshire cat over the tip he'd just been given.

Progressively aware of the pins and needles that she was doing a balancing act on, Isabelle didn't really remember the trip home. It was a blur wrapped up in gauzy hopeful anticipation.

Conversation was erratic.

"Do you think your mother's asleep yet?" she asked, trying not to sound as eagerly hopeful as she was.

Brandon glanced at the backlit clock in the dashboard. It was approaching ten.

"Hard to say. I can remember a time when she used to get up at ten to attend some party in her honor back when she was the toast of Broadway."

"When she did *Love Me Sweet* and *The Lucky Rainbow*," Isabelle put in, nodding her head.

Brandon spared her a glance. Several weeks into this and she was still impressing him. "You really *are* a fan," he marveled.

Why did he seem so surprised? "I said I was. Your mother's part of a dying breed." He probably took that for granted, seeing as how he'd grown up anchored inside of his mother's reality. "There aren't many stars of her caliber left."

Brandon laughed, shaking his head. "I can see why she gets along so well with you. Just don't let her get carried away or, before you know it, she'll have you dragging out her scrapbooks and albums for her own private performance of show-and-tell."

At least here she was one up on him. "Too late, she already has," Isabelle told him. "As a matter of fact, it was a couple of weeks ago."

"And still you're here," he pretended to marvel.

She'd been thrilled to death to see the scrapbooks that Anastasia had saved over the years.

"Actually, I considered it an honor. She told me that she doesn't share those pictures with everyone."

"No," he agreed. "Most people can usually outrun her when she's lugging those scrapbooks out."

"You're being irreverent," Isabelle pointed out, "but I've got the feeling that you're really very proud of your mother."

That had been a given for a long time. "Well, yeah, I am," he admitted. "She's come a long way and managed to get to where she was against a lot of impossible odds. And even though most of my life was spent being raised by strange women with heavy accents, Mother did make it a point to try to be there at bedtime to tuck me in whenever she wasn't filming half a continent away." An affectionate, understanding smile curved his mouth. "Anastasia Del Vecchio was the best mother she could be, under the circumstances." And then he laughed softly to himself.

Isabelle wanted to share his moment, his memory, if only for a little while. "What?" she prodded.

"Mother often brought her characters home. I was never sure if the woman tucking me in would have a southern accent, or talk to me about a new 'case' she was bringing to trial—" He saw the slightly confused furrow on Isabelle's brow and explained. "One season my mother played Katharine Hepburn's role in a revival of *Adam's Rib*." He grinned. "I guess I'm lucky she never played Joan Crawford in that bio movie based on her life. You know the one." He paused, trying to remember the title.

Isabelle remembered for him. *"Mommy Dearest."* She smiled as she shook her head. There was staying in character and then there was going way too far. She was fairly confident that, despite her tendency toward the dramatic, Anastasia knew where to draw the line.

"I doubt if she would have taken a wire coat hanger to you, no matter how deeply into the part she submerged herself," Isabelle told him with conviction.

He liked the fact that Isabelle admired his mother. Half the women he'd dated didn't even know who his mother was. Their sphere of knowledge was very small, limited to the current disposable faces on commercial television, otherwise known as tomorrow's has-beens, he thought. Isabelle was different. But he already appreciated that.

Turning, Brandon pulled into the driveway. He cut off the engine and pulled up the handbrake.

It was on the tip of her tongue to ask him why he was stopping when she looked around and answered her own question.

Somehow, they had managed to arrive. The trip hadn't seemed nearly long enough.

She decided that the kiss on the dance floor had some pretty lasting lethal effects. Why else would she have lost track of time like this?

Peering through the windshield, she looked up at the house. There were lights on all over, but that didn't mean anything. Anastasia liked a well-lit house, said the darkness made her feel sad, so Brandon made a point of leaving them all on while his mother was awake.

"Gives new meaning to 'keep a light burning in the

window,'" Isabelle commented as she got out of the vehicle.

"The power company loves my mother," Brandon acknowledged. "She uses enough electricity to light up her own midsize country," he added with a weary sigh. At this point, there was no changing Anastasia or "teaching her a new trick," and he had pretty much resigned himself to that. He'd told Isabelle the other day that he was a firm believer in the AA credo about having the strength to live with the things that couldn't be changed. His mother was one of those "things."

"She still might be asleep," he told her as he quickly disarmed the security system so that he could unlock the front door. They had to hurry before it engaged itself again. "After you," he gestured her inside the house.

Isabelle slipped in and then stood in the foyer, listening for the sound of clicking slippers. Though Anastasia was still relegated to wearing the white cotton surgical stockings for another week, she had balanced out her displeasure by beginning to work her way back into her high heels, her footwear of choice "because they make my legs look long and slender" she liked to boast.

"And at my age," she'd just recently added, "I need all the help I can get."

There was always a pregnant pause at the end of that pronouncement as the legendary star of stage, screen and television waited to be told that she didn't need that much help and that she was still as beautiful as ever.

Victoria had gotten very good at picking up the cue and responding. But with her gone, the task, Isabelle felt, fell to her.

She couldn't help wondering if Victoria would be back from camp when it came time for her to leave the household or if she'd have to tender her goodbyes after the fact.

There was only a week left to the six weeks she'd agreed to when she first came to work with Anastasia. The cutoff point had been a firm goal with no wiggle room. She'd either be well enough to go, or not.

Isabelle had no doubts that Anastasia would be well enough. Beneath the dramatic displays of vanity, the over-the-top glitter and the carefully applied makeup was a very stubborn woman who refused to cry "uncle" in any manner, shape or form. There'd been a couple of minor temporary setbacks, but for the most part, the actress had forged full steam ahead.

That made it her duty, Isabelle thought, to act not just as the woman's physical therapist, but her coach and have Anastasia not just ready, but raring to go no matter what.

Isabelle knew as she walked into the family room, it was also her duty to make sure that Anastasia didn't jeopardize her health *while* she put forth this almost superhuman effort to get ready. It amazed her just how resilient and strong a woman of Anastasia's age—and what she would guess had been a life of sheer excess—really was.

"I don't think she's—"

Whatever Brandon was about to say to her, and she had a feeling it was about his mother, he never got to voice because Anastasia chose that moment to make her entrance from a room she'd dubbed "the library" because there were a number of books on its shelves.

"Ah, you're finally home," Anastasia declared. She made a show of looking at her watch. "Getting in a little late for a school night, wouldn't you say, dear?" The question was addressed to Brandon.

"It's summer and Victoria's away at camp," he pointed out.

"Camp," Anastasia repeated with a disapproving shake of her head. "Camping out with bugs and furry creatures that eat with their hands."

"Paws," Brandon corrected, amused.

That only made his mother shiver. "Disgusting," she declared. "And completely uncivilized. I don't know why you sent her."

He hadn't *sent* Victoria anywhere since she was six years old. Wherever she went—school, dance classes, art lessons—she went willingly, because she wanted to.

"I didn't *send* her, Mother. She went because she wanted to go. It was her idea, remember?" he reminded his mother. "She thought she'd have fun. And besides, Marisol was going," Brandon added. The two girls had been fast friends since they'd sat next to one another the first day of kindergarten.

Anastasia moved her shoulders in a careless shrug. She never surrendered when it came to an argument, even if she was proven wrong. She knew how to turn things around to seem as if she'd been right all along.

"Well, I suppose there's that, too," the actress conceded loftily. "At any rate, solitude is highly overrated," she said, waving her hand about to include the whole house. "I've gotten accustomed to the sound of you rattling around, making noise." She drew herself up, as if preparing to go to her room. "Now that you're home, I can go to sleep."

Amused despite himself, Brandon couldn't help asking his mother, "Just what do you do when you're in your own home?"

Anastasia offered him a very sly smile in response.

"Who says I'm alone there?" And with that hanging in the air between them, she majestically turned away and withdrew.

"She really is something else," Isabelle said, admiration echoing in her voice as she watched the actress disappear around the corner leading to her bedroom.

"Yes, she certainly is," Brandon agreed. "And someday science will figure out exactly what that 'something' is." And then his demeanor shifted as he turned his attention to her. "But enough about my mother." He did a fairly good imitation of a radio announcer from a more dramatic, bygone era. "I believe when we last saw Isabelle and Brandon, she was in his arms and he was having a difficult time controlling his desire for her."

Isabelle laughed, amused. She would have never expected this lighthearted, boyish side of him. "Are you planning on narrating everything that happens between us?" she asked, doing her best to maintain a straight face.

"Probably not." He brushed his lips against each cheek, then dusted her eyes with one tiny kiss apiece. "Suspense thrillers are my forte, not romantic scenes, remember?"

She smiled up into his eyes as he pulled her into his arms. "Oh, I wouldn't exactly say that," she contradicted. "You seem to have a very natural aptitude for romantic scenes."

"Nice of you to notice," he told her, continuing to shower her face with tiny, arousing kisses. "I think you should know that no matter what I'm doing, I always try to top whatever I've done before."

Right at that moment, her heart launched into a triple beat. "Well then, in the words of the immortal Bette

Davis, I guess I'd better fasten my seat belt because it's going to be a bumpy night."

"Don't bother fastening anything," he instructed. "I'll only have to unfasten it."

Brushing his lips against hers one final time, he then took her hand and led her upstairs to his room, which he'd been dying to do all day.

Chapter Fifteen

"Physical therapist by day, goddess of love by night. You really are the total package, aren't you?"

Brandon's breath warmed her skin as he made his half teasing observation.

They were lying in his bed, his arm tucked protectively about her, her nude body still throbbing from the thrill of making love with him just a few short minutes ago. He stroked her hair and pressed a kiss to the top of her head. She hung on to the glorious euphoria that had been wrapped around her for all she was worth.

She heard him laugh softly. "If I pull something because I give myself too much credit for flexibility, you can fix me and put me back together again. Total package," he repeated with admiration.

"As long as you're not Humpty Dumpty, I can give it my best shot," she replied.

The heat of his body reached out to hers, stirred her. Whispered of another go-round.

She could literally *feel* herself aching for him.

"Your best is more than enough for me," Brandon told her.

At times it's almost too much, he added silently. Isabelle could wear him out and then have him begging for more in an incredibly short amount of time, he marveled. What kind of power did this woman have over him? She'd turned a perfectly normal man with ordinary needs into this insatiable creature whose appetite just insisted on growing. This new man had nothing in common with the man he'd *thought* he was.

Brandon inhaled the fragrance in her hair.

Obviously he'd thought wrong. He was so much more. If he was wrong about one thing, he could very possibly be wrong about other things as well, he told himself as his arm tightened around Isabelle.

For instance, he could be wrong about the way he viewed his future, he speculated. Until Isabelle had entered his life with her sunshine and her laughing eyes, he'd thought he knew exactly the way the rest of his life would unfold. He'd work, attend parties and be there for both his daughter and his mother. The idea of another woman permanently installed in his life was utterly out of the question. Once on the marriage-go-round had definitely been more than enough for him. Besides, he'd reasoned, most likely, he'd make the same mistake over and over again and pick someone like Jean.

Isabelle was *nothing* like his first wife.

Consequently, for the past couple of weeks he'd begun to have second thoughts about his overall view of the rest of his life in general, and about his view of marriage specifically.

Most of all, he'd rethought the concept of giving up. After all, he hadn't just thrown his hands up when he'd received his first rejection slip, hadn't said he'd given it his best shot and stopped trying.

No, like a glutton for punishment, he kept coming back for more. And more. Until he got what he was after. A publishing company that gave him a one book contract and a chance to prove himself.

That, of course, had led to other books, other contracts. After that humble beginning, he never looked back.

Why would he approach marriage any differently? He had picked the wrong person the first time, that was all. Looking back, that had been over thirteen years ago. He'd been an untried kid of twenty at the time. He was far more sophisticated now, more discerning, more versed in analyzing characters and the motivation that went into them.

Moreover, he knew what he was looking for in a life partner, and he was well aware of the danger of just jumping in with both feet without assessing the situation first.

He was assessing it now, and he *liked* what he saw. Liked the thought of facing each day knowing that Isabelle would be somewhere around within that day—and within all the days to come.

That didn't automatically mean that the thought of marriage didn't make him nervous. And it didn't mean that the prospect of getting married again, of trusting someone else with the care and keeping of his heart, was not scary as hell, because it was.

SCARY in big, bold capital letters.

But, risk nothing, gain nothing—wasn't that what he'd told Victoria more than once? If it was an edict he felt was good enough for his precious daughter, it sure as hell was good enough for him.

All he had to do, he thought, looking at the woman tucked into the crook of his arm, was get up the courage to ask Isabelle.

But he had a little time before he had to work on getting up his nerve. Right now, Isabelle was still very much in his life and would continue to be as long as his mother needed her.

He found himself torn. He certainly wanted his mother to bounce back to her incredible old self, but her reaching that plateau would do away with the need for Isabelle's presence.

Brandon smiled to himself. Who would have thought that he'd wind up being a very strong advocate for slow-and-steady winning out in the long run, like the tortoise in the fable?

An uneasiness began to undulate through Isabelle. Brandon had been quiet for a while now. Longer than usual. As a matter of fact, this was the longest he'd ever been quiet without the excuse of dozing off.

Asleep, there was a reason for the silence. But he wasn't asleep. And he wasn't talking.

What was he thinking?

Her uneasiness grew, slipping through her veins, putting out the fire that had just been there a few short seconds ago. She went from hot to freezing cold in one heartbeat.

Something was wrong. She could *feel* it.

Isabelle vacillated between coming right out and asking Brandon what was wrong and ignoring the entire thing.

But that was no way to move ahead. Ignorance was *not* bliss and anyone who believed that was an idiot. Not knowing was the basis for constant uneasiness and the onset of paranoia.

Still, a little voice inside her voted for ignorance. It whispered that ignorance was better than being forced to face a harsh truth that could shatter everything good at this moment.

So, rather than lie there, speculating, having thoughts bouncing about in her head as if she was the ball being lobbed back and forth in a continuous game of tennis, Isabelle turned into him, bringing her nude body up closer against him and sealing her lips to his. With instant results.

The way she saw it, she was buying herself a little time, reveling a little longer in the fairy tale world that they had spun for themselves.

The sudden maneuver caught Brandon completely off guard.

But not for long.

As ever, he prided himself on being able to rise to the occasion. This time was no different.

"You're going to wear me out, you know that, don't you?" he asked with affection echoing in his voice.

She responded with a laugh and drew him even further into their fiery new world.

He went willingly.

"You know, when you first came, I had my doubts about you," Anastasia told Isabelle frankly.

She had just completed an exercise she had found too grueling and next to impossible a few short weeks ago. This time, much to her satisfaction, it had all gone perfectly. She'd begun at one end of the exercise room and made it all the way over to the other end, not just in record time, but without losing the tension in the band that Isabelle had placed around her lower thighs.

Of necessity, she'd waddled like a duck, but a very graceful duck, she liked to think. And that, to Anastasia, meant that she had passed the "course" set before her. From here on in, any exercises she faced would be the regular kind, meant to keep her body flexible and limber, something she liked to think kept her youthful as well.

"Oh?" Isabelle asked, her curiosity aroused. "What kind of doubts?"

Anastasia shrugged in that vague, dismissive way of hers. "I knew you had to know your stuff. After all, you did get a degree in physical therapy. But I didn't think you were woman enough to ride herd over me—" She saw the surprised expression on Isabelle's face and watched it melt into bemusement. "Yes, I know I can be, let's just say 'difficult' by some standards—"

"You, Anastasia Del Vecchio, are difficult by anyone's standards," Isabelle interjected with genuine affection. The woman was an experience like no other, and she would always be grateful for the opportunity to be with her. "But it's also what makes you uniquely you," Isabelle concluded with complete conviction.

Anastasia appeared exceedingly pleased with the assessment.

"Glad you could see that. Anyway," she said getting back to original point, "I didn't think you could make me do these silly little exercises, but you could and you did and I'm obviously the better for it." That was said a bit grudgingly. "Thank you," she declared, then surprised Isabelle even more by pulling her into her arms and awarding each cheek with a kiss. "You have done me—and my public—a tremendous service."

"I'm glad I could be of help," Isabelle replied, doing her best to look serious.

Inside she suddenly struggled with a tidal wave of bittersweet feeling that threatened to completely overwhelm her.

Somehow, she managed to keep a smile on her face and an upbeat note in her voice, but it was definitely *not* easy.

This is the end, a voice in her head whispered. *It's over. The fairy tale you've been gliding on is about to break apart. Time to get back to the real world, Cinderella.*

Isabelle took a breath. She might as well know it now. "When do you go on tour, Anastasia?"

"They leave the day after tomorrow." She tossed the words in her direction as if they were of no consequence. As if they didn't have the power to blow up a carefully crafted world, spun entirely out of sugar. "Thank God, I got in a little rehearsal time before my accident—not that I don't know the play cold," she added with her customary, undaunted confidence. "You'll come to the show when we bring it back to L.A.?" the actress asked her suddenly.

Isabelle drew in a breath, as if that could somehow protect her heart, put a shield around it and forced a smile to her lips. "Wouldn't miss it for the world," she promised.

The woman graced her with a satisfied, beatific smile. "Good, then I'll be sure to leave a ticket at the box office for you."

A ticket.

A single, lonely sliver of paper to denote her status in life, Isabelle thought. Single. Forever.

Funny, she had resigned herself to that before she

came here, making peace with it. Knowing it was better than living in a constant heightened state of dread, subconsciously waiting to be betrayed, the way her father had betrayed her mother.

But being here, being a part of this family, a family she had come to care about a great deal, had changed everything for her, at least temporarily. Living here had made her dream and yearn for something more. Something richer.

She'd even begun to think that it was possible...

That, idiot, was your big mistake. How could it have been possible? He's Brandon Slade, for God sakes, and you're...just you.

Stop it, she ordered herself sternly. *You knew it would be like this when you signed on. This is a world-famous writer. What do you have to offer the man he can't get somewhere else? Nothing.*

Her old life was calling and she had to go. It was good enough for her once, it would be good enough again. And very soon, all this would just seem like a dream, a wonderful, euphoric dream.

"Oh, my," Anastasia said, moving about her room. "There's a thousand things I have to see to before I leave. And I have to call Tyler," she announced suddenly. "Tyler Channing is the director." She tossed the name carelessly toward Isabelle. "He's been pulling out what little hair he has left, worrying whether or not I'll be ready to join the tour in time. He has this little contract player on standby," she confided, then snorted at the very thought of someone else taking her place. "Well, she can just keep on standing by because, thanks to you—" the actress beamed at her "—I'm ready. Ready to bring down the house," she declared with relish.

In the world of Anastasia Del Vecchio, there was no such thing as half measures.

"God, I don't know where to start," Anastasia said to herself, turning about in a complete circle as she surveyed every inch of her room, obviously trying to decide where to begin.

Isabelle slipped out of the room as the actress continued making plans, obviously happy to reclaim the life that had once been hers.

Too bad we can't all feel that way, Isabelle thought.

She sincerely doubted that the actress even noticed that she'd left.

Now what? Isabelle wondered as she walked down the hallway.

The house was empty.

Brandon was in Hollywood for a good part of the day. He and his powerhouse of an agent, Maura, were meeting with a producer who had expressed no small interest in bringing one of Brandon's earlier books to the movie screen.

For the first time since she'd arrived here, the large house felt hauntingly empty to her. It was an omen, Isabelle decided. Time for her to pack up her things and leave.

The thought of saying goodbye brought a lump to her throat. With her luck, the words would probably get stuck there if she tried to say them. She wasn't very good at taking her leave. She lacked the gift of knowing what to say and how to say it. Slipping off into the darkness was more her style.

It was just better this way. She certainly didn't want Brandon to feel awkward in her presence. Didn't want him to feel he had to say something to her about the time they'd spent together. And she *certainly* didn't want him to feel that he had an obligation to stay in touch with her.

That was something she would have wanted to have happen because he *wanted* to, not because he felt he *had* to.

And even so, even if he told her that he wanted to stay in touch, who was to say that she would actually welcome that? Wasn't she the one with an underlying fear of commitment? A fear of commitment because she was afraid of the disappointment that seemed to go with it?

She vividly remembered hearing her mother cry when her mother had confronted her father. It was the only time she could recall her mother displaying any sort of emotion. Except for that one time, her mother had always seemed distant, frozen inside and utterly inaccessible.

There was something to be said for that, Isabelle thought as she closed the door to the guest room where she'd lived these past six weeks, closed it for the last time.

If you're inaccessible, if you have an impenetrable shield wrapped all around you, nothing could possibly hurt you. There were a lot of worse things than that, she mused as she slowly took her clothes off their hangers and folded them one by one, then placed them into her suitcase.

Maybe, if she kept busy enough, if she moved fast enough, Isabelle told herself, she could outrun the pain that hovered over her like a bullet seeking its target.

Waiting to destroy her.

Blinking back tears, she stepped up her pace, doing her best to give her theory a good run for its money. It was all she had.

* * *

Brandon was flying.

For once, that sensation didn't involve the needle on his speedometer straining toward numbers that were frowned upon by police departments in all fifty states.

That was because he was flying emotionally.

The meeting with the producer had gone not just well but extremely well. And now it looked as if he would see the characters he'd "given birth to" take on three-dimensional form across the big screen. Saying words that he had put into their mouths.

Hell, he would have paid them for the honor. Instead, they were paying *him*. Not only that, but the amount of money bandied about between the producer and his barracuda of an agent was almost sinful. The last time he'd heard amounts like that was when he was a kid, playing Monopoly with one of the many nannies his mother had hired for him.

He felt almost guilty accepting the money.

Almost.

Even adjusting for inflation, it was way more than enough to send Victoria to the world's most expensive college three times over when the time came. Send her to college and buy her a small country of her own as well, he thought with a grin.

But that wasn't even the best part of it all. He'd finally, *finally,* gotten started working on his next book. It had been rocky at first, but he was going like a house afire now. So much so that he'd felt as if he had to tear himself away just to attend this meeting today.

His renewed fire was all thanks to his new muse.

All thanks to Isabelle.

Talking to her the other night had made everything fall into place, made it all come into focus.

By nature he was ordinarily an upbeat sort of person, but having her around had wound up making his very soul sing.

That, my boy, is because you've finally given yourself permission to be in love.

There was no getting around that, he thought—not that he really wanted to. He'd forced himself to admit it. He was in love. And being so made all the difference in the world.

He was anxious to make it official as soon as possible. He wanted to tell Isabelle how he felt about her. Wanted to declare his feelings out loud so that he could go forward and start making plans. Important plans. Plans not just for the two of them but for all three of them because Isabelle and Victoria had a bond, as well.

The very thought of that made him incredibly happy. He suspected that Victoria felt exactly the same way about Isabelle as he did.

Well, maybe not *exactly* the same way, he amended with a wicked grin, but close.

Brandon pressed down on the accelerator, in a rush to get back home. Finally, he could go forward with his life. He no longer believed that the best was behind him, he thought as he pulled up before his house. The best was yet to be.

As he got out of his car, Brandon was vaguely aware that Isabelle's car wasn't parked at the curb or in the driveway either.

What a time for her to pick to run an errand, he thought, just the slightest bit crestfallen.

He was going to have to hang on to his enthusiasm for a little while longer, he told himself. Until she got back.

He hoped he could hold out.

Chapter Sixteen

"Well, you're looking pretty pleased with yourself," Anastasia commented to her son when he walked into her room.

Or rather, to his reflection in her mirror, which was what she was looking at as she finished carefully arranging her hair. Done, she turned around to face him and crossed to her bed which was currently buried under mounds of her clothing.

"You're just in time to help me decide. Which color is more flattering? The turquoise?" She held up a dress that was clearly not meant for daywear. "Or the hunter green?" She switched to another garment, one that was shot through with silver threads, and held it up against her torso.

"The turquoise," he told her. Unable to hold the news in any longer, he shared it with her. "And I've just sealed a deal to have *The Thrill of the Hunt* made into a movie."

About to remove the last articles of clothing from her closet, Anastasia stopped in midstep and whirled around to look at Brandon. There was genuine pleasure in her eyes. "Oh, how wonderful, Brandon!" Ever the competitive actress, she automatically asked, "Do you think there's a part in it for me?"

"Depends," he said, brushing a kiss to her cheek. "Can you play a tough as nails L.A.P.D. detective in her early thirties?"

"She's that old?" Anastasia lamented, then waved her hand, dismissing the subject. "Maybe I'll just let someone else get it."

He saw her glancing in the mirror, examining her profile. Some things never changed, he thought fondly. "That's very thoughtful of you." Belatedly, the chaos on her bed—and the opened suitcases—registered. "What are you doing?"

"Packing, darling." She laughed indulgently. "You'd think after all these years of watching me do it, you'd recognize it when you saw it."

And here it was, the weather forecast for his parade. Was it merely going to rain, or was there a flash flood in the offing? "But you weren't going to leave until your physical therapy program was over."

"Exactly." Anastasia stopped packing her clothes and went through the motions of taking a curtain call bow. "It's over. I am officially 'as good as new.'" She allowed a contented sigh to escape. "Isabelle said there was nothing else she could do for me."

Why was there this uneasy, queasy feeling burrowing into the pit of his stomach?

He was jumping to needless conclusions, Brandon

told himself. "Speaking of Isabelle, do you know when she'll be back?"

Anastasia looked at him blankly, waiting. When he didn't continue, she asked, "No, when?"

"I'm asking you," Brandon stressed, struggling to keep this strange, swiftly-growing agitation he was experiencing from getting out of hand.

Ah, the mighty confirmed bachelor has fallen, Anastasia thought, well satisfied. She'd seen that look before, on the faces of the men who told her they were in love with her. "How should I know? Her work here is done."

That was exactly the answer he didn't want to hear. "Then she's not coming back?"

As far as Anastasia was concerned, she was playing her part beautifully, seeing as how she was improvising her dialogue as she went along.

In true motherly fashion, she put her hand to his cheek. "Darling, is there something wrong with your attention span? I just said I was 'good as new.' Isabelle's accomplished what she came here to do. I'm sure she'll be moving on to another assignment. She might even be starting right now," Anastasia speculated.

He was having a very hard time wrapping his head around this. "And she left here—for good—without saying goodbye?"

"Well, she said it to me," Anastasia informed him, as if she was the primary one who counted in this scheme of things. "But I suspect that was only because our paths crossed at the front door. I think she just wanted to slip quietly away without making a fuss." She smiled. "You know how unassuming Isabelle can be when it comes to herself."

He knew. He also saw her leaving like that as something different than not wanting to "make a fuss." He saw it as running out on him.

Just as his ex-wife had.

Except that back then, he knew why Jean had run out on him. She'd told him in no uncertain terms. She wasn't cut out to be a mother and didn't want to be tied down by either a baby *or* a husband.

It was different with Isabelle. She was everything he wanted in a woman, in a life partner—or at least he *thought* she was everything he wanted.

Now he didn't know.

What he *didn't* want was someone who couldn't be counted on. Someone who literally turned around and ran after all but pledging her heart to him.

Or had he misread that, too?

"What's the matter, dear?" Anastasia asked, playing the concerned mother for all she was worth. "You look as if you've just lost your best friend." Deliberately pretending that she was misinterpreting the reason for the look on his face, she crossed to him and took his chin in her hand. "Don't worry, darling, I'll be back to visit you and Victoria regularly. I promise."

He forced a smile to his lips, removed her hand and turned it so it was palm side down. In the fashion of gallantry of centuries gone by, he pressed a kiss to her hand.

"I know you will, Mother." He let her hand go and stepped back. "I'll get out of your way so you can finish packing. Let me know when you want me to take the suitcase to the front door for you."

"Won't be for a while yet, dear."

His mother's voice followed him out into the hallway, but he hardly heard her.

She was gone, he thought, numbly placing one foot in front of the other.

Isabelle was gone.

Gone, just like that.

Without a word, without so much as a nod. Gone as if those nights they'd spent together hadn't meant anything to her. As if their days together, the drives, that moment in the rain on the beach, hadn't meant anything to her.

Without his knowing exactly when, exactly how, Isabelle, with her lighter-than-air laugh and her quiet determination, had become embedded in his life, in his family. And then, just like that, like some Band-Aid being ripped off, she'd torn herself away and was gone.

His mind spinning every which way at once, he thought of going out and finding her. Of shaking her and shouting at her for doing this to him.

For lying like this to him without saying a single word.

Damn it, he upbraided himself, clenching his fists at his side, how could he have been so hopelessly stupid to let himself get ensnared like this? How could he have been so—

He had a book to work on, he told himself sternly. He had no time for any grieving, dramatic or otherwise. It was time to submerge himself in his work, the way he'd always been able to do before, and forget about everything else.

Forget about lips the flavor of strawberries and eyes that seemed to shine whenever she looked at him. Forget about skin the texture of cream and a body—

This wasn't helping, Brandon berated himself. At this rate, he would talk himself into a state mental institution by evening.

"Write, Slade. It's what you do," he ordered sternly as he marched into his office. "At least she didn't *take* that away from you."

Brandon closed the door behind him and willed his mind to focus.

Isabelle tried, she really, really *tried* to summon up her former enthusiasm. She needed it in order to do her work. She needed it so that she could find just the right way to motivate her clients.

But try as she might, she just couldn't seem to find it. It was as if every last drop of enthusiasm had evaporated on her. Along with her sense of humor, her energy and forget about her mind. That seemed to be long gone.

At various times of the day and evening, she'd find herself suddenly "stuck." Lost in a motion or a thought that went no further. She looked like an adult playing the old children's game of "statue" where players would "freeze" in a position when the word was suddenly called out.

Except that no one was calling out anything. It was just her. She seemed utterly unable to function properly. Not without her heart. And that was gone.

It had been a week like this. A whole terrible, debilitating week.

She *had* to snap out of it.

Zoe had already said that one of the clients had complained about her. Well, not exactly complained, but they'd wanted to know if there was something "funny" about her because she was acting so very strangely, getting lost midsentence. Staring off into space.

Of course, her present client, Bobby Johnson, a major league baseball player who was on the team's disabled list because of a pulled hamstring, didn't seem to mind her slipping into a trancelike state for a minute or so at a time. That was probably because he thought it had to do with him.

Currently, Bobby was in one of the firm's therapy rooms, expounding on how hard it was to live a normal life, surrounded by women who insisted on following him everywhere he went, even to the men's room at the gym he frequented.

"But I guess that all just goes with the territory," he concluded with as phony a sigh as she'd ever heard. "That really feels good," he commented, then suddenly he swiveled around on the padded table he'd been lying on. He pulled his towel around himself as he sat up, leaving it deliberately loose in order to serve as an un-spoken invitation for her benefit, Isabelle's couldn't help thinking. "Hey, you doing anything after this?" Bobby asked. He didn't wait for her to answer, but just assumed it would be what he wanted to hear. "Because if you're not—"

"She is."

Both she and the technically disabled infielder turned to look at the man walking into the room.

Isabelle's heart leaped into her throat, all but singing. "Brandon."

The baseball player was scowling as darkly as Isa-belle was smiling. "Hey, this is my time with Izzy," he declared indignantly. "Who the hell are you?"

"I'm Brandon Slade, the writer." He added the last part when the seminaked man on the table stared at him as if he was beneath him.

Bobby frowned, clearly at a disadvantage. "You write books?" Apparently replaying Brandon's name through his head, he shook it. "Never heard of you."

Brandon's less than genuine smile never faded. "Well,

that makes us even, because I've never heard of you, either."

While he followed football and basketball fairly regularly, he'd never cared for the game deemed to be the great American pastime. In his opinion it moved much too slowly.

Unable to take it a second longer, Isabelle interrupted the exchange. "Brandon, I'm working," she pointed out unnecessarily. "What are you doing here?"

He would have thought that was self-explanatory. This "invasion" was uncharacteristic of him, but then, so was what he was feeling.

He'd given up pretending he didn't care where Isabelle was or that she'd left without saying a word. Rather than just call where she worked, he'd come down to see her in person. He'd found Zoe in the front office, which had saved him the trouble of trying to charm information out of the receptionist. Isabelle, she'd told him, was here, in the back, working with a client.

She'd then proceeded to surprise him by asking, "Do you need to see her right now?"

He hadn't even had to think about his answer. "More than you could ever know."

The woman had nodded, seeming to understand what he was going through. "Tell Isabelle I'm sending in another therapist. Go do what you have to do." Her eyes had been shining as she'd added, "Good luck."

He could have hugged her. Digging into his pocket, he'd left a hundred-dollar bill on the desk. "In case the guy complains about the interruption."

And then he'd gone in search of the room.

When his heart had accelerated at the sound of her voice, he'd known he hadn't made a mistake coming here. They belonged together.

"What do you think I'm doing here?" he said in response to her question. Taking her hand, Brandon firmly pulled her toward the door. What he had to tell her had to be said without an audience. Opening the door, he looked at the ballplayer over his shoulder. "Game over, baseball boy. You're cured," he announced.

For once Bobby Johnson was utterly speechless. They left him that way.

She might not have had a word for Bobby, but she had plenty for Brandon. "Brandon! You can't just interrupt a session like that."

"I'm not interrupting it," he informed her, crossing the threshold with her in tow. "I'm ending it. Don't worry, I paid for his session, so he can't complain. Zoe's getting another therapist to come in and take your place." Looking back at the fuming baseball player, he called out, "Don't worry. If you feel shortchanged, there's another therapist on her way." Facing Isabelle again, he said, "Let's go."

Not wanting to cause a scene, she waited until she was outside the office—her sister was conveniently gone, and the receptionist looked at her wistfully as they passed by the front desk.

Once the door had closed and they were out in the hall, she abruptly stopped walking and yanked back her hand.

When he turned around to look at her, Brandon saw that she was furious.

"You had no right to embarrass me like that," Isabelle fumed.

He'd never seen her angry before, and for a moment, he just took it in. And then, as in a poker game, he matched her. And raised her one.

"If I embarrassed you, I'm sorry. But *you* had no right

to just walk out on me, on *us* like that," he amended, thinking of what Victoria would say once she returned from camp and heard what had happened. "Without so much as a damn word! Like I was just someone you'd passed on the street."

Don't you know that you'd never be just like someone I'd pass on the street? That you were and are so very special to me? Too special, she underscored.

Out loud, she merely said, "I didn't want to make a big deal out of it."

"Well, by not saying anything, you did. You made a hell of a very big deal out of it," he informed her, all but yelling into her face. He struggled to get the better of his anger. Shouting at her wasn't going to bring her around.

Isabelle couldn't wrap her head around the logic of his words. "I just assumed you would have preferred it that way. Quietly," she emphasized.

His eyes were dark with suppressed anger. "What I would have 'preferred,'" he informed her, "was a chance to talk to you."

She took a deep breath, telling herself that she wasn't intoxicated by the very scent of him. That her heart wasn't beating harder than a bongo drum, racing to a strange, exotic beat. That this rush was normal for someone in an argument.

She ran the tip of her tongue along her very dry lips to moisten them. "Well, you're here now. Talk."

He should just go. Ignore her. Not let her know that she'd succeeded in shredding him into teeny-tiny little slivers. That was the only way to save face. To save his pride.

But the truth was, he didn't give a damn about his

pride. What he gave a damn about, now that he'd found her, was Isabelle.

He struggled not to take hold of her shoulders, afraid he'd wind up hurting her by holding on too tightly. "Damn it, Isabelle. Was it all one-sided? All that time together, was I just there by myself? Fooling myself?"

She was having trouble catching her breath, centering her thoughts. Trouble staying where she was instead of throwing herself into his arms and just holding on for as long as he'd let her. She'd missed him more than she had ever thought possible.

Taking in a shaky breath, she tried to sound calm as she asked, "About?"

"About us!" he shouted. "About you. About you caring." He took a breath. "Damn it all to hell, Isabelle, you can't just leave like that. I need you."

Isabelle shook her head. It sounded too good to be true. Or maybe she had just imagined she'd heard him say that. *Ached* for him to say that. "You need me?" she heard herself asking, praying that if this was a dream, a hallucination, she wouldn't ever wake up.

"That's right, I need you," he all but shouted, struggling to get his voice under control. "I need you very much." His voice softened, and he smiled down into her face. "As does my mother and Victoria. Nothing's going to be the same in the house until you decide to take pity on us—on *me*—and come back."

"Come back as what?" she asked. "Your mother doesn't need a physical therapist. Anastasia's going away on that cross-country tour. And Victoria's still at camp—I talked to her yesterday," she told him before he had a chance to question how she knew his daughter's current location.

"You're right," he answered honestly. "My mother

doesn't need a physical therapist. What she needs is a daughter-in-law." His eyes took her prisoner. "Any suggestions? Know anyone open to taking on that position?"

Again, Isabelle stared at him, this time utterly dumbfounded. She couldn't have heard him right—could she?

The ensuing silence throbbed in his ears like a thunderous heartbeat. It was far from a comfortable silence. "Look, I get it. You're scared. Well, I'm scared, too. We can be scared together," he proposed. "And tell each other that there's nothing to be scared about. Your father might have played around on your mother—"

Her eyes widened as she stared at him, stunned. "I never told you that."

"No, you didn't trust me enough to let me in on that," he conceded.

She didn't understand. "Then how—?"

"Zoe told me. Nice woman, your sister," he said with approval. "I like her."

How could her sister have betrayed her like this? Made things known about her without asking first? "Don't get used to her. She's on borrowed time."

He laughed, shaking his head. "You're unconventional, Isabelle, I'll give you that. I guess it's one of the things I love about you."

The all-important phrase echoed in her head. "One of the things you lo—" She blinked, stunned beyond words. "You love me?"

"Hell, yes, I love you. What do you think we're talking about?" he demanded.

"I don't know. You lost me when you said you liked my sister."

"I like your sister," he repeated patiently. "But I *love*

you." He took in a deep breath. Waiting. Praying. "You have anything to say to me?"

Adrenaline raced through her like a gathering lightning storm. She was utterly surprised that she was still standing. "You're crazy."

He laughed, waving the words aside. "Okay, anything to say to me other than that?"

She couldn't stop smiling. Her face refused to relax. "Maybe I love you, too."

He eyed her. "Maybe?" It was going to be all right, he thought. She needed to take baby steps, and he was all right with that. As long as the steps ultimately led to him.

She felt as if her heart was bursting. As if what she had always secretly wanted was suddenly being granted after all this time. "All right, all right, all right. Yes, I love you. Satisfied?" she cried.

"Getting there. Now, about that vacancy that I mentioned. You know, the one for a daughter-in-law for my mother—"

There went her heart again. "Then you *are* saying what I think you're saying?"

"I am if you think I'm proposing." Right on cue, Isabelle's mouth dropped opened. "I thought you deserved an unconventional proposal." His eyes were already making love to her—asking her to give him the answer he needed to hear. "But if you don't like that one, I can rewrite it until I find one that you do like." Opening his jacket, he reached into his pocket for a small scratch pad and his pen.

She put her hand on top of Brandon's, stopping him before he got carried away. "There's no point in rewriting it. Why don't you just ask me?"

Was that all it took? Just asking her? "Because I

didn't think it would be that simple. In a world of plain butterscotch pudding, you're custard cream."

That had to be the strangest compliment she'd ever received. But it was definitely a compliment, and she loved it.

Loved *him*.

Isabelle couldn't help wondering what she was letting herself in for. And part of her could hardly wait to find out.

"Ask me," she coaxed in a soft whisper.

God but he loved her. Even so, he couldn't resist teasing her. "To be my physical therapist?"

Isabelle was beginning to catch on to the way his mind worked. She shook her head. "Ask me the other thing."

He stopped teasing and grew very serious. "Isabelle Sinclair, will you marry—?"

"Yes," she cried before he had all the words out. "Yes, I'll marry you."

Throwing her arms around his neck, she knew she'd just given him the right answer. It was the right thing to do. The only thing she *wanted* to do with all her heart. Brandon *wasn't* like her father. He wasn't going to disappoint her. Wasn't going to break her heart as her father had broken her mother's. She was betting her own on it, but she'd always been a safe better, and this, she was certain, was definitely a sure thing. And now that she'd finally gotten out of her own way, she saw that clearly.

He smiled down into her face. "Right answer," he told her before he kissed her and set his world back on track again. "Oh, by the way," he said just as his lips had brushed seductively against hers, "I wasn't just talking a minute ago. I really do love you. More than I ever thought possible. Hey," he cried, upset by her reaction, "I didn't mean to make you cry."

"Happy tears," she told him. "These are happy tears. Because I love you, too," she added, then sealed her mouth to his before he could find another footnote to add to the occasion.

Epilogue

The applause was like life-giving water to a thirsty flower. She stood there, bathed in it, absorbing it as she and the rest of the cast took yet another curtain call. Their fourth.

But as wonderful as it was, as much as she had really missed the sound of instant, gratifying feedback, Anastasia had to admit, in the privacy of her own soul, that something, a small but viable component, was missing from her life these past three months that she had been on the road, touring with the play. A component that interaction with the other members of the cast and crew—some old friends, others brand-new acquaintances—as entertaining as it often was, could not adequately replace.

Which was why, as she sat in her small, private dressing room going about the task of turning herself back into Anastasia Del Vecchio, legendary icon, and her cell phone rang, she immediately stopped what she was doing and reached for it.

Hoping.

A glance at caller ID as she flipped the phone open brought an instant wide smile to her lips. Love was evident in each word as she asked, "Hello, darling, how are you?"

"I'm good, Gemma," the girl on the other end of the call answered. "Did you knock 'em dead again tonight?"

A deep, throaty chuckle met her granddaughter's question. Grandmother though she was, she was also part living legend, a fact she never forgot. "Do you have to ask?"

"No," Victoria readily agreed. "I don't. You always knock 'em dead."

"You were always my very best audience, sweetheart." Anastasia looked at her watch. It was after eleven. "Forgive me for making grandmother noises, my love, but shouldn't you be in bed, asleep?"

"I wanted to wait until your show was over before I called," Victoria answered evasively.

Anastasia was instantly alert. Bohemian-like though she had been for most of her life, there was a very strong mother-grandmother streak alive and well within her heart. It rose to the foreground, blotting out everything else. "Why? What's wrong."

"Nothing's wrong, Gemma. I just wanted to call you as soon as I heard."

"Heard what?" She had never once lost patience with her granddaughter, but she felt herself coming close to the edge now.

Instead of answering, Victoria asked a question of her

own. "Do you think you can come home three weeks from Saturday?"

Anastasia blew out a breath. "Victoria, you grow more and more like your father every day. Now what is going on?" She wanted to know. "*Why* do you need me to come home? Is it your father? Has something happened to Brandon?"

"Well, yes," Victoria hedged. "Something's happened and it does involve Dad, but not like you think."

Her head suddenly filled with a variety of dramatic scenarios, none of them good, Anastasia assured her granddaughter, "Trust me, you have no idea what I'm thinking. Now, what's going on, Victoria?" she demanded with the full range of her powerful voice. She was a force to be reckoned with.

"Dad's getting married!" Victoria cried happily, the news all but bursting out of her. "To Isabelle," she told her in case there was any doubt. "They just told me. It's going to be at Maura's house because it's so big and all," she went on breathlessly, referring to her father's literary agent. "But they said they won't have it if you can't make it. Tell me you can make it, Gemma. I've never seen Dad look this happy before," she added.

Anastasia laughed shortly. As if anything could keep her away. "Of course I can make it. My understudy is watching me like a hawk, hoping I'll fall off the stage and break the other hip so that she can go on in my place. She'll be thrilled if I take a few days off. But why didn't Brandon or Isabelle call me themselves?"

Just as she asked the question, Anastasia heard her phone beep, telling her that another call was coming in. She quickly glanced at the screen for confirmation. "Well, speak of the devil. It's your father," she told Victoria.

"Oh. He's probably calling to tell you the news. Don't tell him I told you. It'll spoil it for him. Act surprised, Gemma," Victoria implored.

"Of course, darling. Acting is what I do best. Now go to bed. Love you."

"Love you, too, Gemma," Victoria said. "Isn't it wonderful?" she couldn't resist asking.

"Yes, darling, wonderful," Anastasia replied, sharing her granddaughter's happiness. She heard Victoria end the call.

Settling back in her chair, Anastasia switched to the incoming call.

"Hello, Brandon," she greeted her son cheerfully.

Raising her eyes, she looked up into the mirror. The woman reflected there was smiling in triumph. And why not, Anastasia silently asked rhetorically. Her son's forthcoming marriage was, after all, at bottom all due to her initially calling Cecilia. She considered the match to be her own personal victory.

Her smile widened as she innocently asked, "So, what's new?"

* * * * *

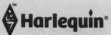 **Harlequin**®

COMING NEXT MONTH

Available June 28, 2011

SPECIAL EDITION

HSECNM0611

USA TODAY *bestselling author B.J. Daniels takes you on a trip to Whitehorse, Montana, and the Chisholm Cattle Company.*

RUSTLED

Available July 2011 from Harlequin Intrigue.

As the dust settled, Dawson got his first good look at the rustler. A pair of big Montana sky-blue eyes glared up at him from a face framed by blond curls.

A woman rustler?

"You have to let me go," she hollered as the roar of the stampeding cattle died off in the distance.

"So you can finish stealing my cattle? I don't think so." Dawson jerked the woman to her feet.

She reached for the gun strapped to her hip hidden under her long barn jacket.

He grabbed the weapon before she could, his eyes narrowing as he assessed her. "How many others are there?" he demanded, grabbing a fistful of her jacket. "I think you'd better start talking before I tear into you."

She tried to fight him off, but he was on to her tricks and pinned her to the ground. He was suddenly aware of the soft curves beneath the jean jacket she wore under her coat.

"You have to listen to me." She ground out the words from between her gritted teeth. "You have to let me go. If you don't they will come back for me and they will kill you. There are too many of them for you to fight off alone. You won't stand a chance and I don't want your blood on my hands."

"I'm touched by your concern for me. Especially after you just tried to pull a gun on me."

"I wasn't going to shoot you."

Dawson hauled her to her feet and walked her the rest of the way to his horse. Reaching into his saddlebag, he pulled out a length of rope.

"You can't tie me up."

He pulled her hands behind her back and began to tie her wrists together.

"If you let me go, I can keep them from coming back," she said. "You have my word." She let out an unladylike curse. "I'm just trying to save your sorry neck."

"And I'm just going after my cattle."

"Don't you mean your boss's cattle?"

"Those cattle are mine."

"*You're* a Chisholm?"

"Dawson Chisholm. And you are…?"

"Everyone calls me Jinx."

He chuckled. "I can see why."

*Bronco busting, falling in love…it's all in a day's work.
Look for the rest of their story in*

RUSTLED

*Available July 2011 from Harlequin Intrigue
wherever books are sold.*

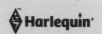